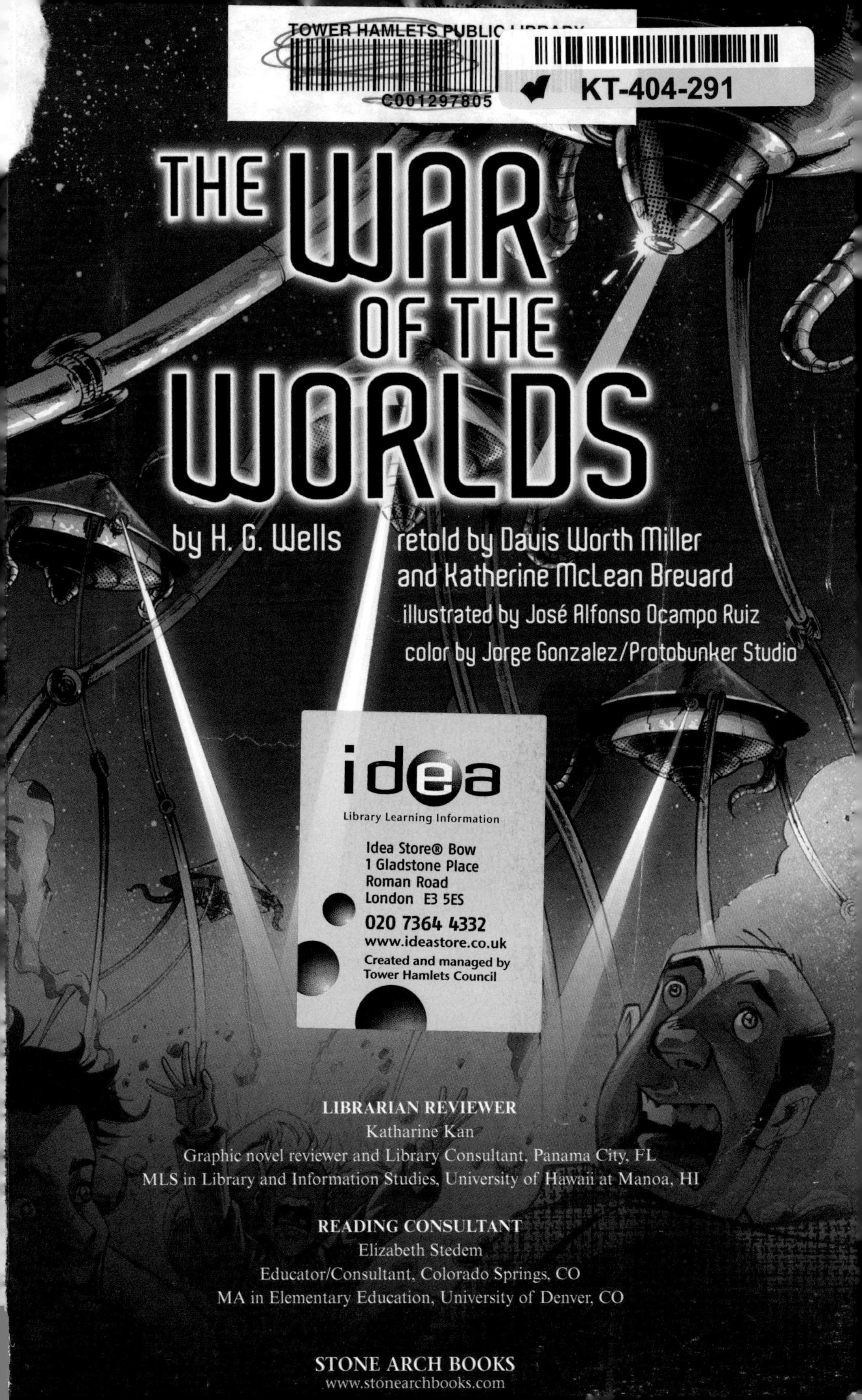

THE WAR OF THE WORLDS

by H. G. Wells
retold by Davis Worth Miller
and Katherine McLean Brevard
illustrated by José Alfonso Ocampo Ruiz
color by Jorge Gonzalez/Protobunker Studio

LIBRARIAN REVIEWER
Katharine Kan
Graphic novel reviewer and Library Consultant, Panama City, FL
MLS in Library and Information Studies, University of Hawaii at Manoa, HI

READING CONSULTANT
Elizabeth Stedem
Educator/Consultant, Colorado Springs, CO
MA in Elementary Education, University of Denver, CO

STONE ARCH BOOKS
www.stonearchbooks.com

Graphic Revolve is published by Stone Arch Books
151 Good Counsel Drive, P.O. Box 669
Mankato, Minnesota 56002
www.stonearchbooks.com

Library of Congress Cataloging-in-Publication Data
Wells, H. G. (Herbert George), 1866–1946.
  The War of the Worlds / by H. G. Wells; retold by Davis Miller and Katherine M.
Brevard; illustrated by José Alfonso Ocampo Ruiz.
    p. cm. — (Graphic Revolve)
    ISBN 978-1-4342-0757-9 (library binding)
    ISBN 978-1-4342-0853-8 (pbk.)
    1. Graphic novels. [1. Graphic novels. 2. Science fiction.] I. Miller, Davis. II. Brevard,
Katherine McLean. III. Ocampo Ruiz, José Alfonso., ill. IV. Title.
PZ7.7.W45War 2009
[Fic]—dc22   2008006250

Summary: In the late 19th century, a cylinder crashes down near London. When George
investigates, a Martian activates an evil machine and begins destroying everything in its
path! George must find a way to survive a War of the Worlds.

Art Director: Heather Kindseth
Graphic Designer: Kay Fraser

1 2 3 4 5 6 13 12 11 10 09 08

Printed in the United States of America

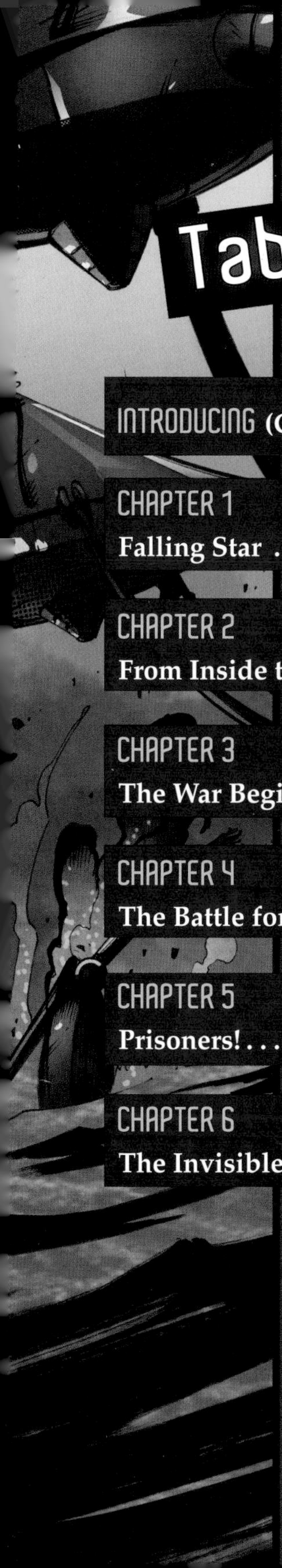

Table of Contents

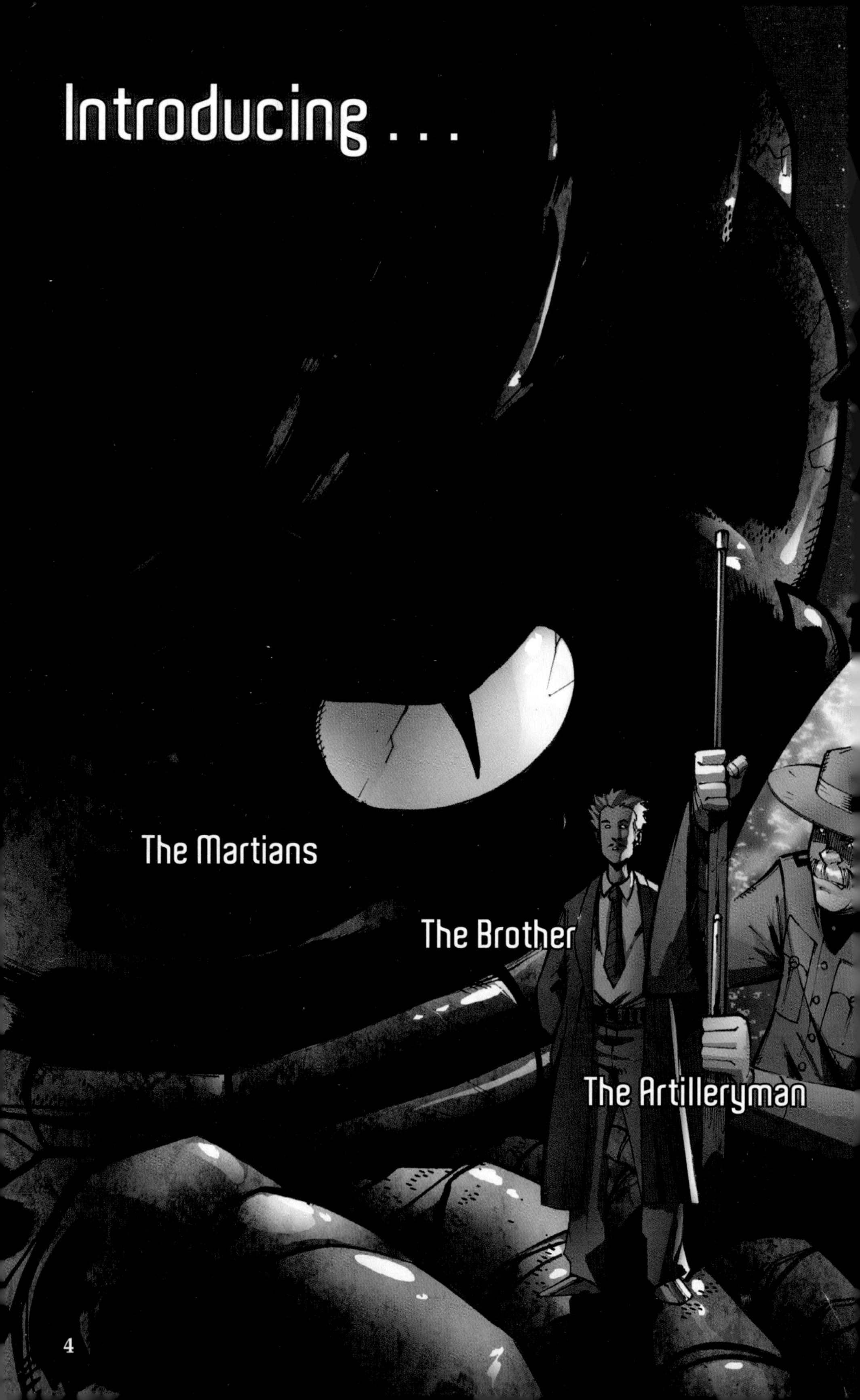
Introducing . . .
The Martians
The Brother
The Artilleryman

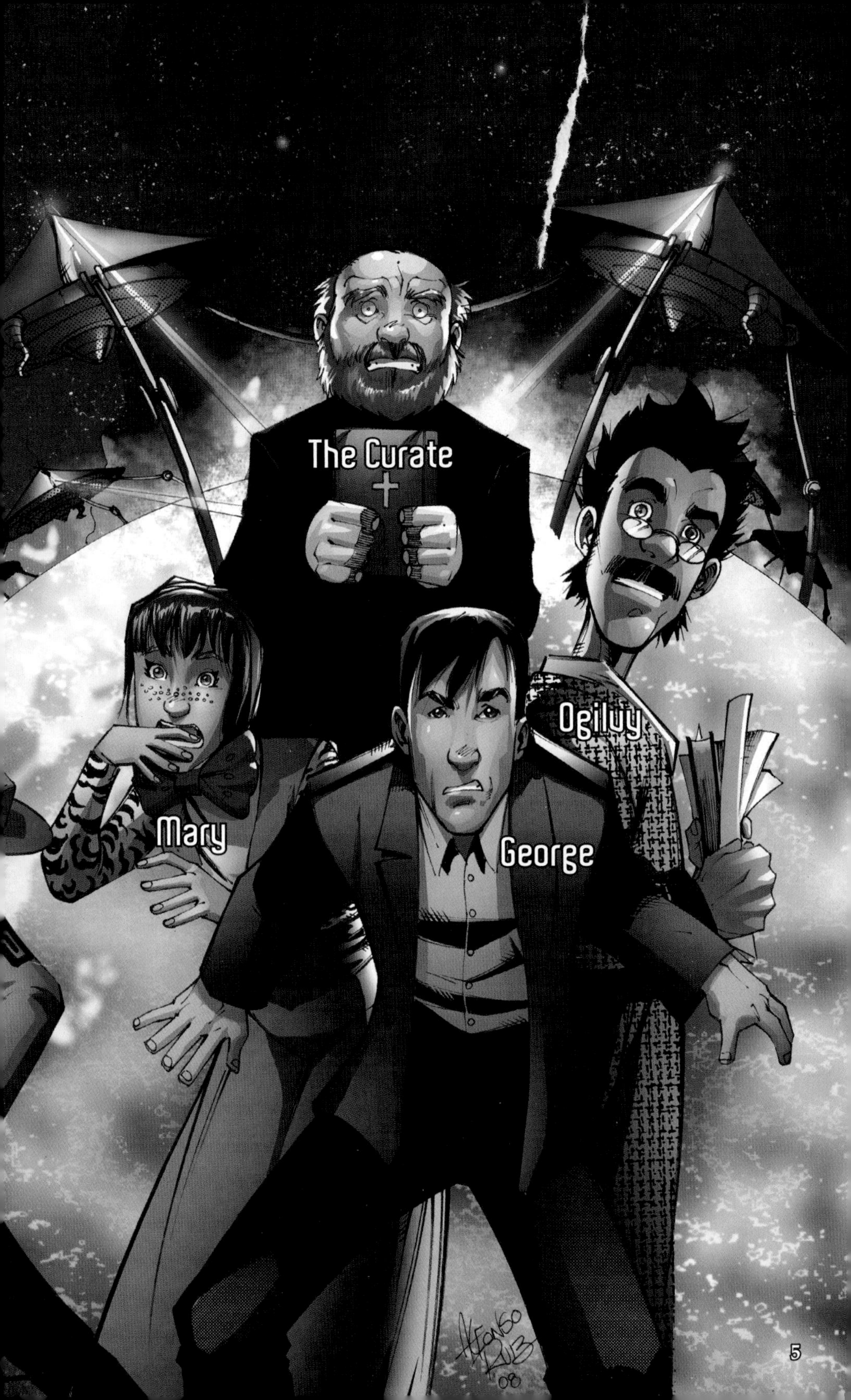
The Curate
Ogilvy
Mary
George

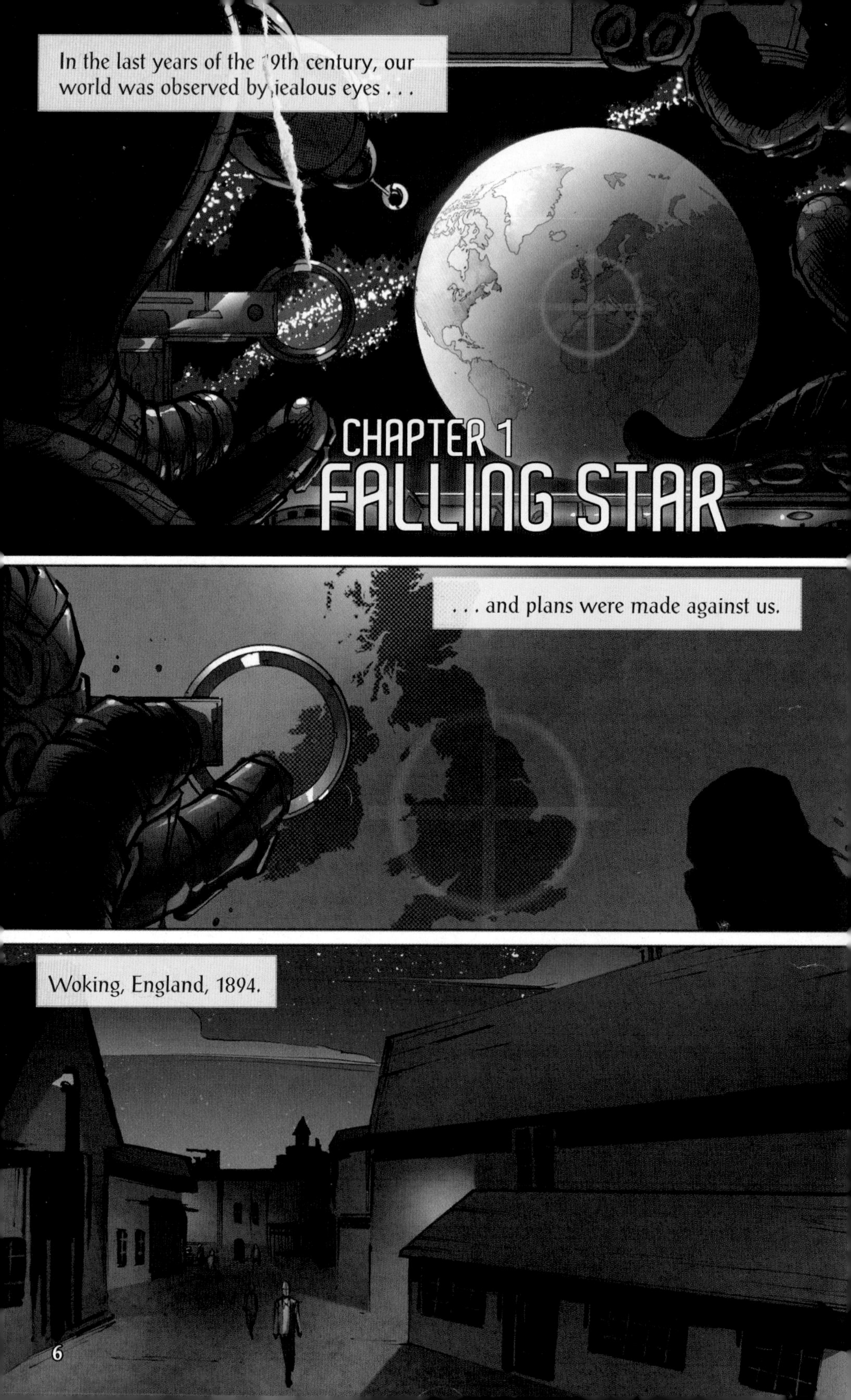
In the last years of the 19th century, our world was observed by jealous eyes . . .
CHAPTER 1
FALLING STAR
. . . and plans were made against us.
Woking, England, 1894.

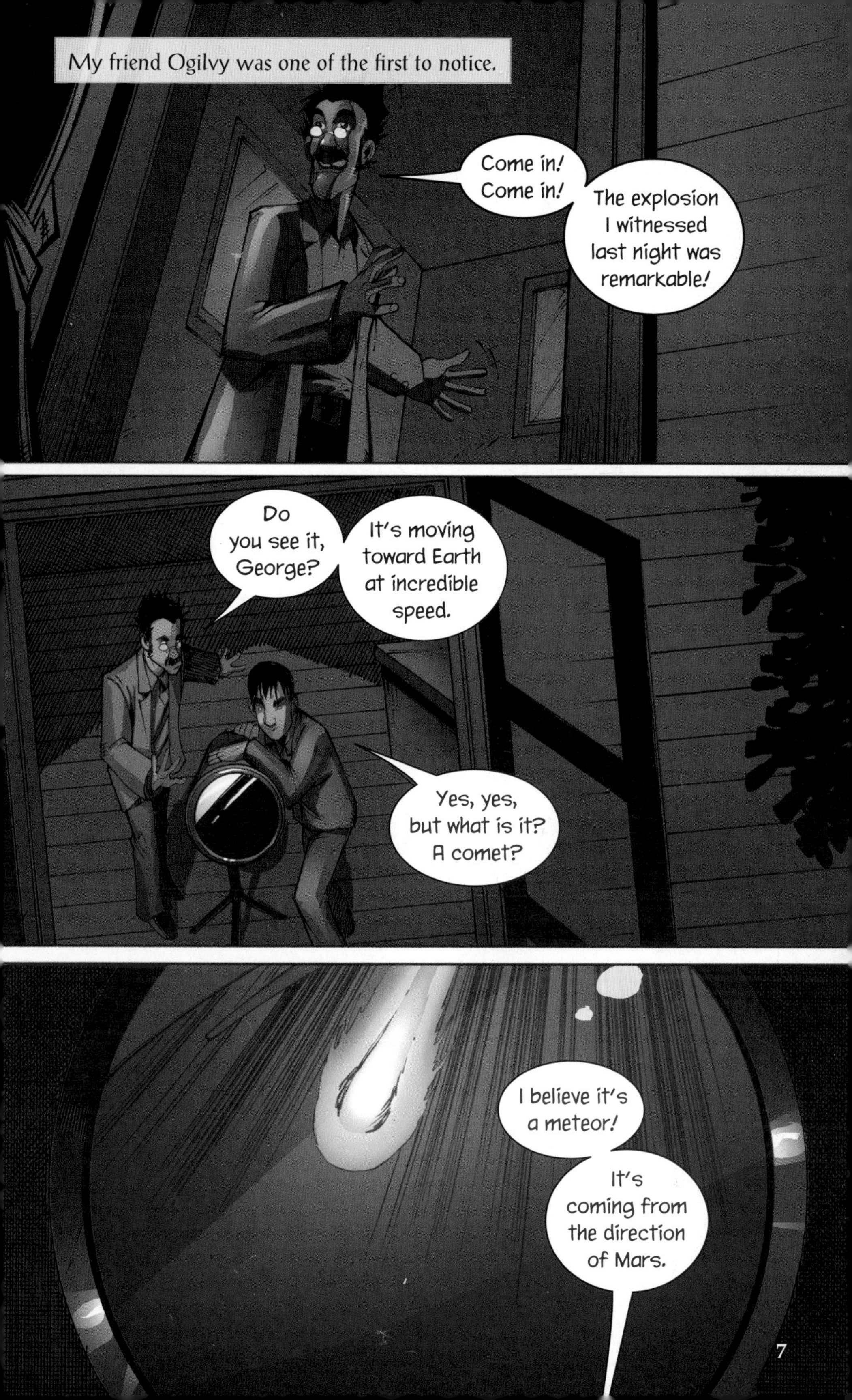
My friend Ogilvy was one of the first to notice.
Come in! Come in!
The explosion I witnessed last night was remarkable!
Do you see it, George?
It's moving toward Earth at incredible speed.
Yes, yes, but what is it? A comet?
I believe it's a meteor!
It's coming from the direction of Mars.

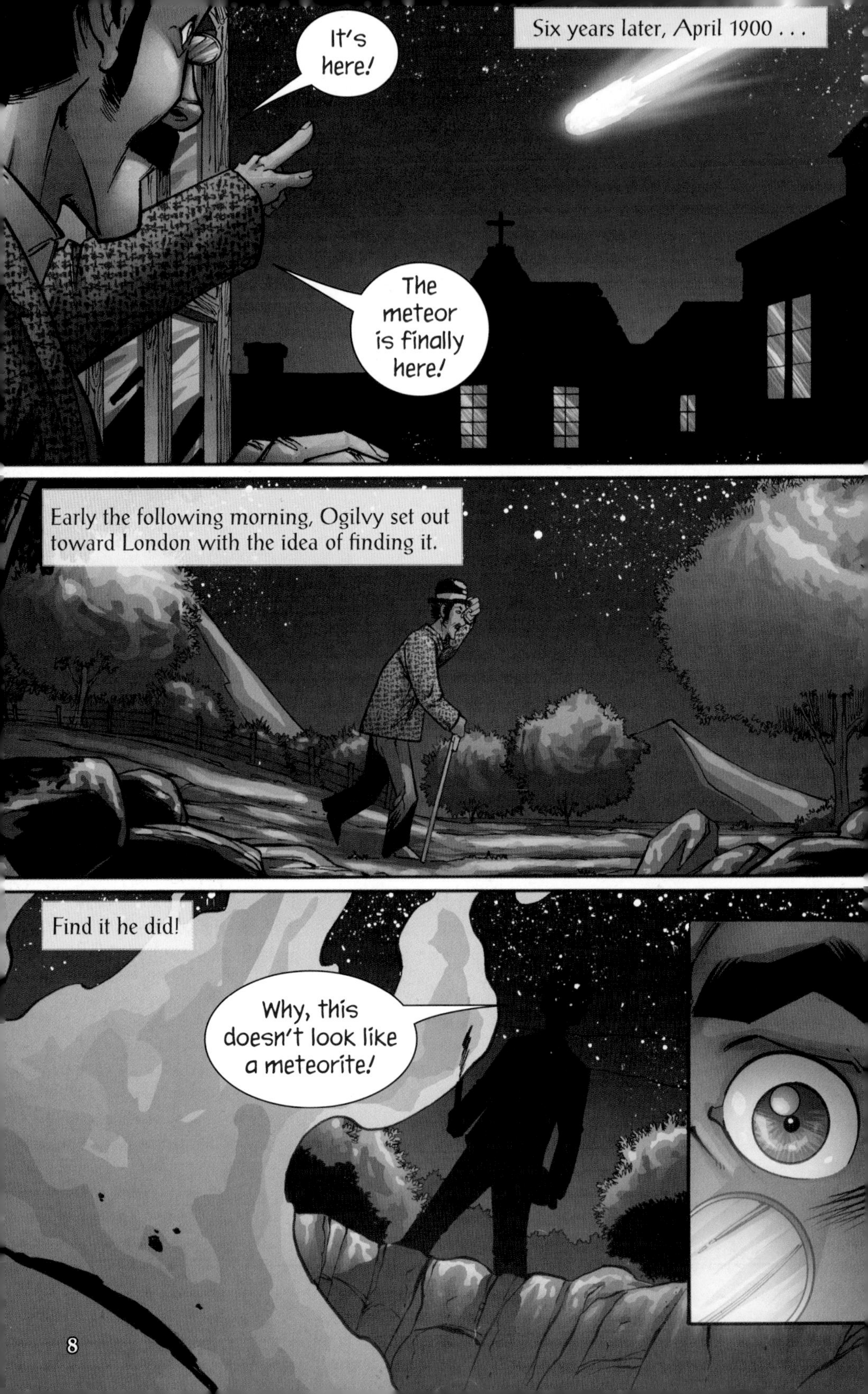
Six years later, April 1900 . . .
It's here!
The meteor is finally here!
Early the following morning, Ogilvy set out toward London with the idea of finding it.
Find it he did!
Why, this doesn't look like a meteorite!

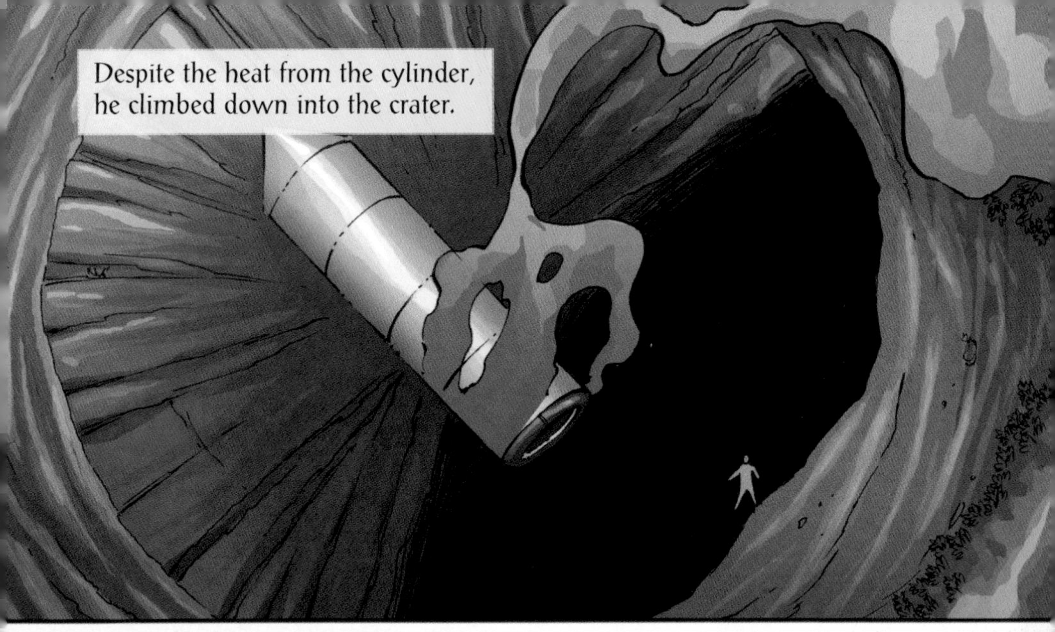
Despite the heat from the cylinder, he climbed down into the crater.

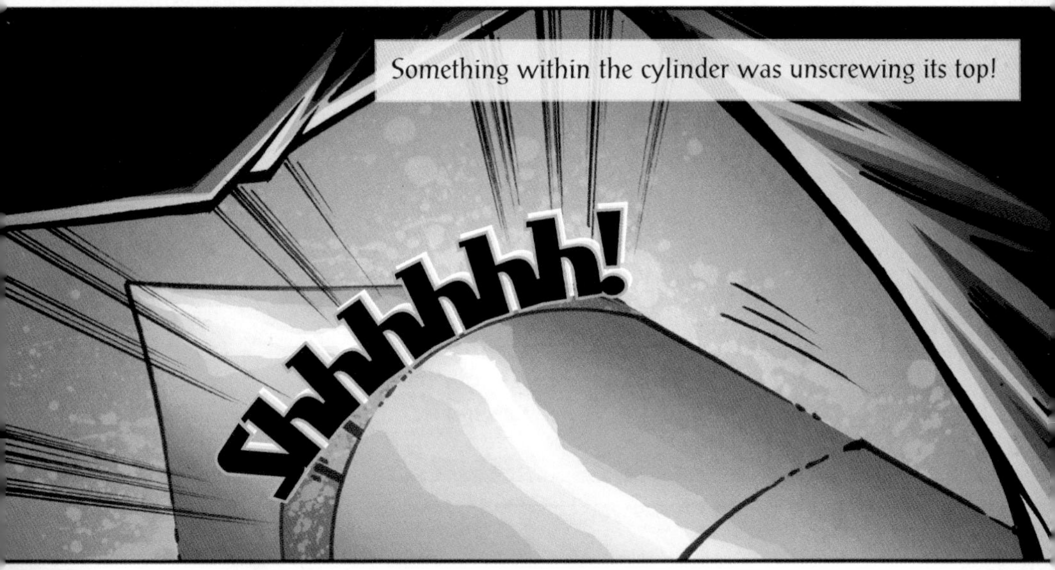
Something within the cylinder was unscrewing its top!
Shhhhhh!

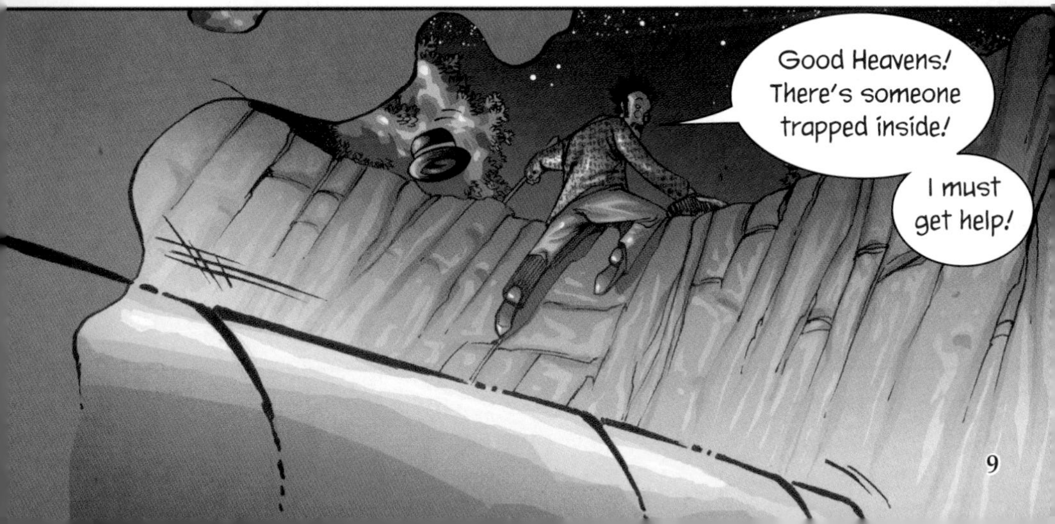
Good Heavens! There's someone trapped inside!
I must get help!

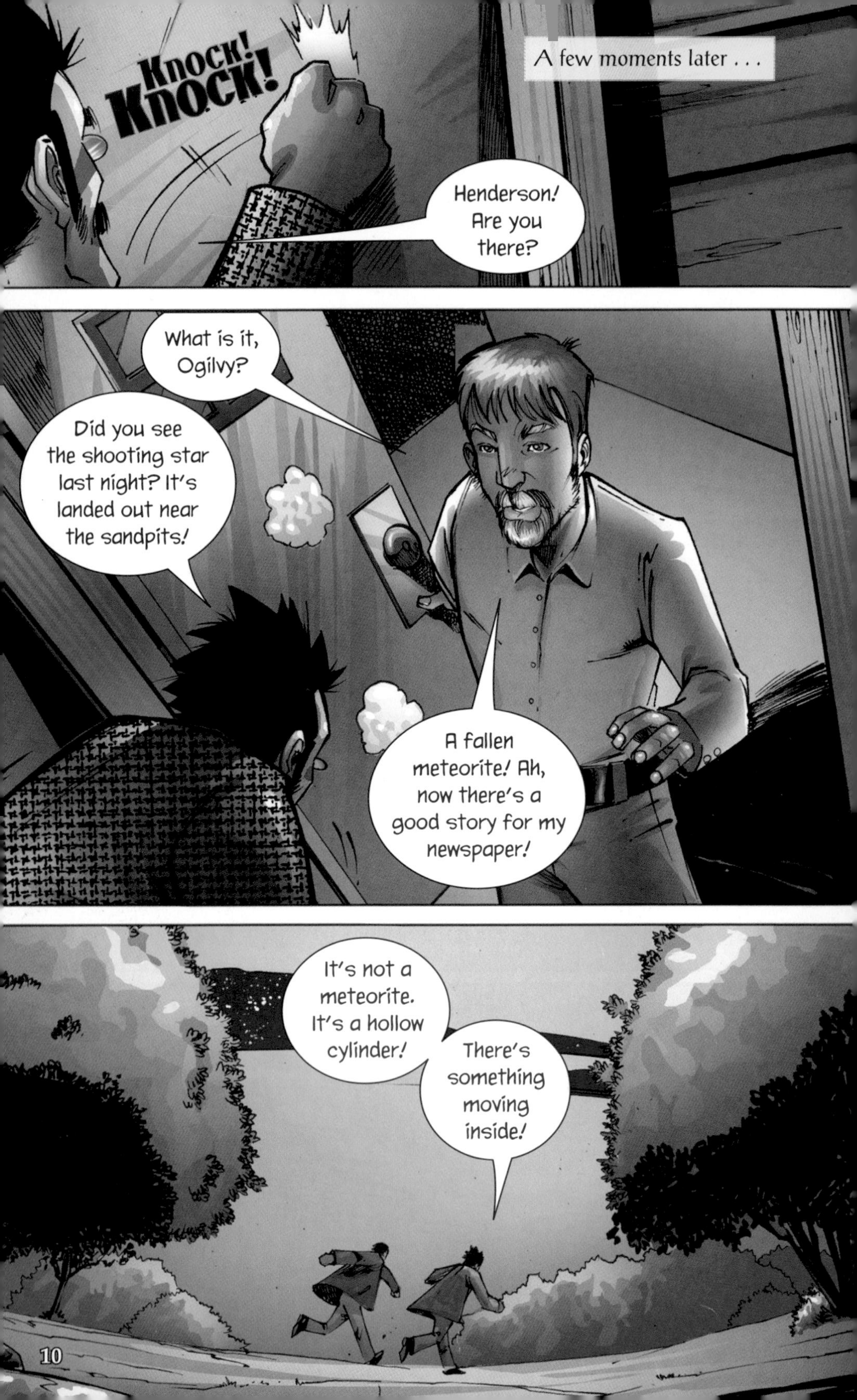
KNOCK! KNOCK!
A few moments later . . .
Henderson! Are you there?
What is it, Ogilvy?
Did you see the shooting star last night? It's landed out near the sandpits!
A fallen meteorite! Ah, now there's a good story for my newspaper!
It's not a meteorite. It's a hollow cylinder!
There's something moving inside!

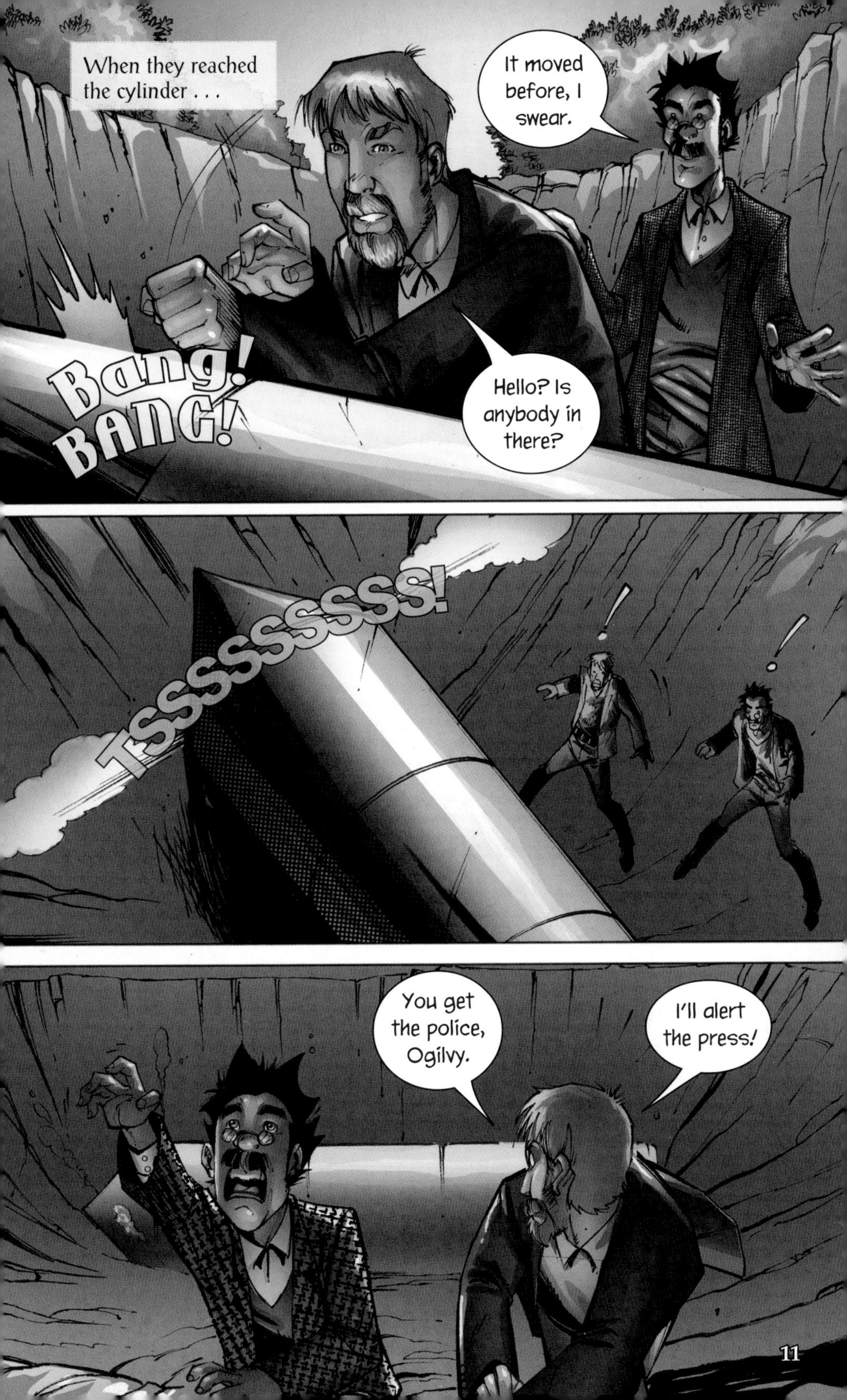
When they reached the cylinder . . .
It moved before, I swear.
Hello? Is anybody in there?
Bang! BANG!
TSSSSSSSSS!
!
!
You get the police, Ogilvy.
I'll alert the press!

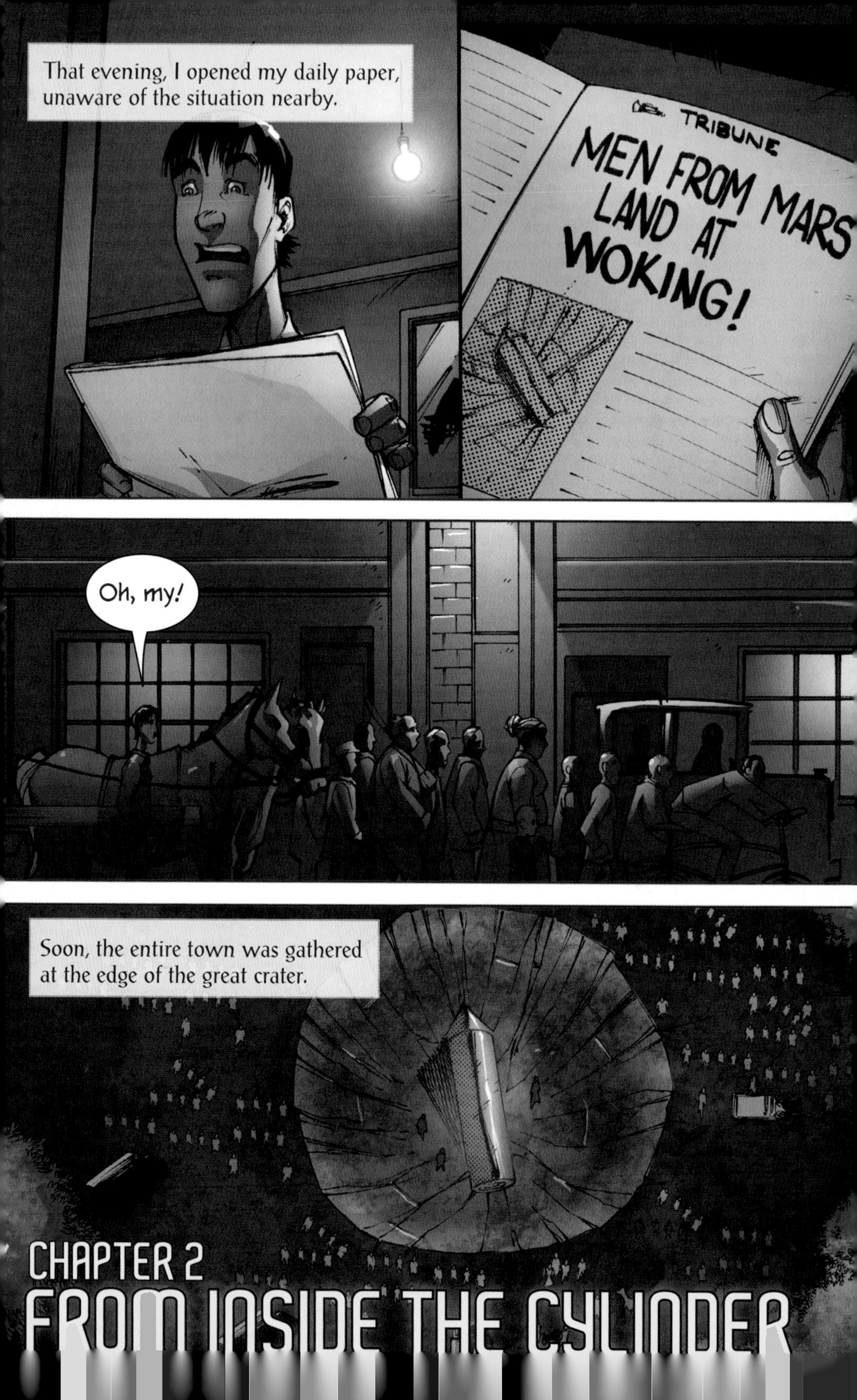
That evening, I opened my daily paper, unaware of the situation nearby.
TRIBUNE
MEN FROM MARS LAND AT WOKING!
Oh, my!
Soon, the entire town was gathered at the edge of the great crater.
CHAPTER 2
FROM INSIDE THE CYLINDER

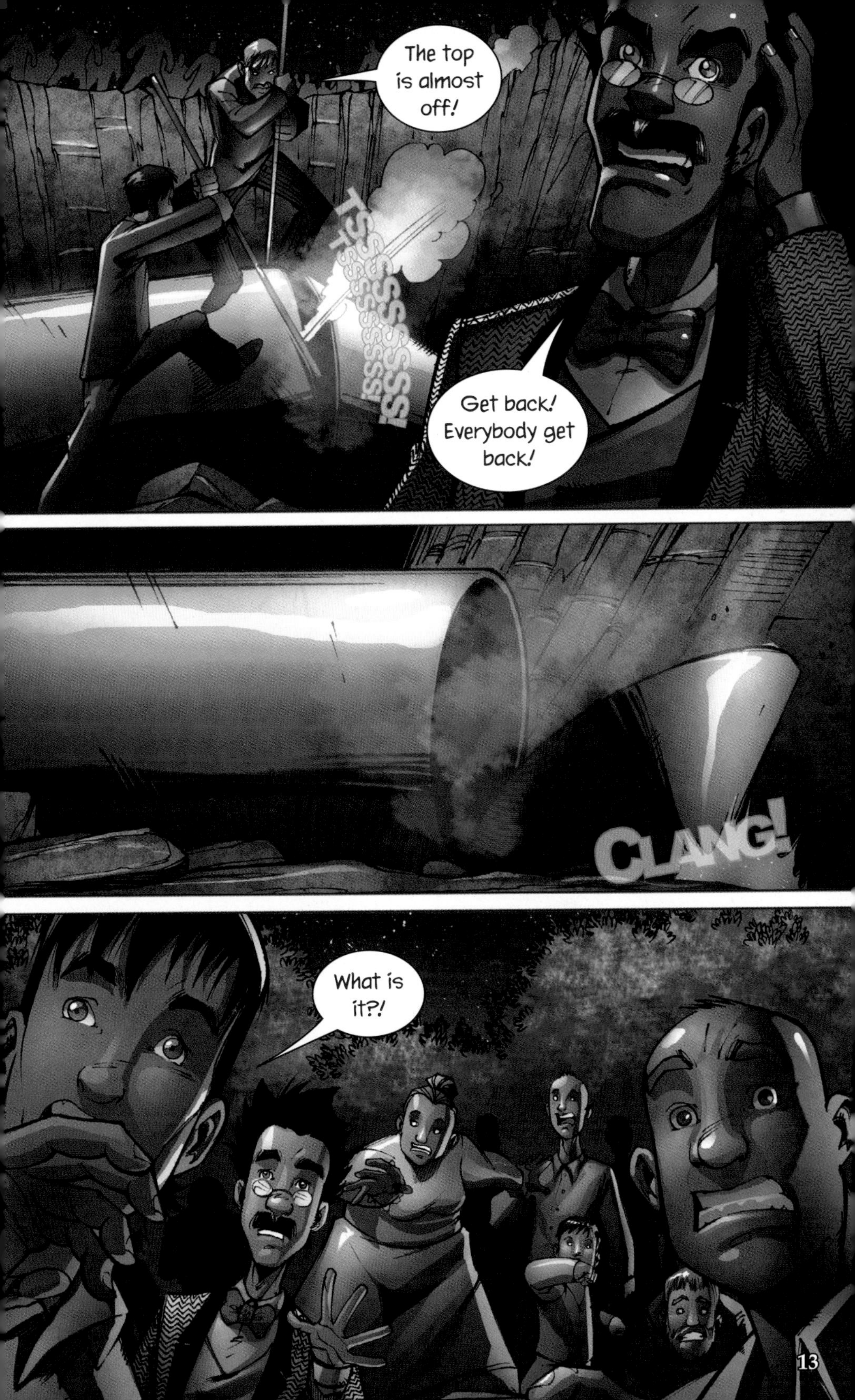
The top is almost off!
TSSSSSSSSS!
Get back! Everybody get back!
CLANG!
What is it?!

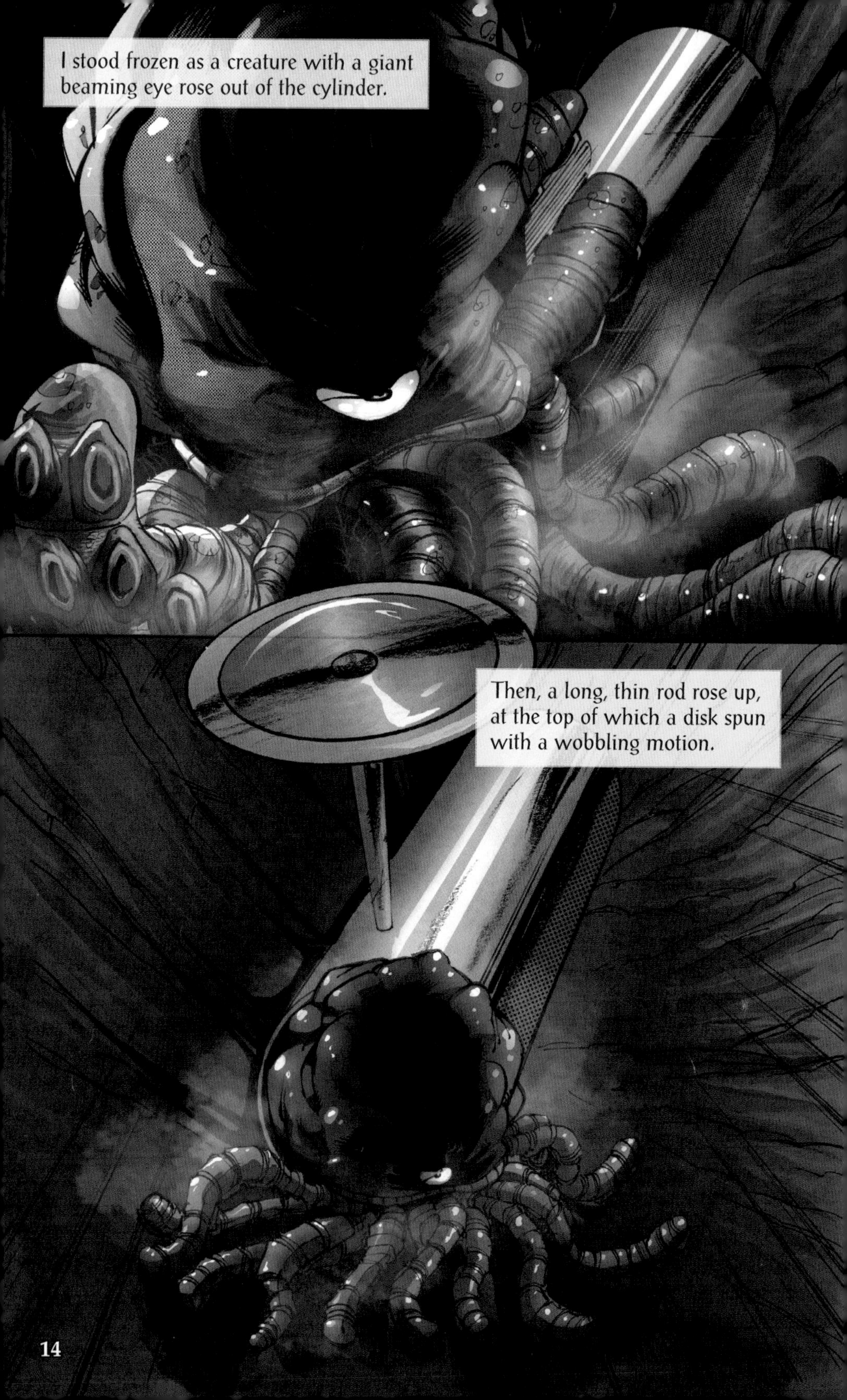
I stood frozen as a creature with a giant beaming eye rose out of the cylinder.
Then, a long, thin rod rose up, at the top of which a disk spun with a wobbling motion.

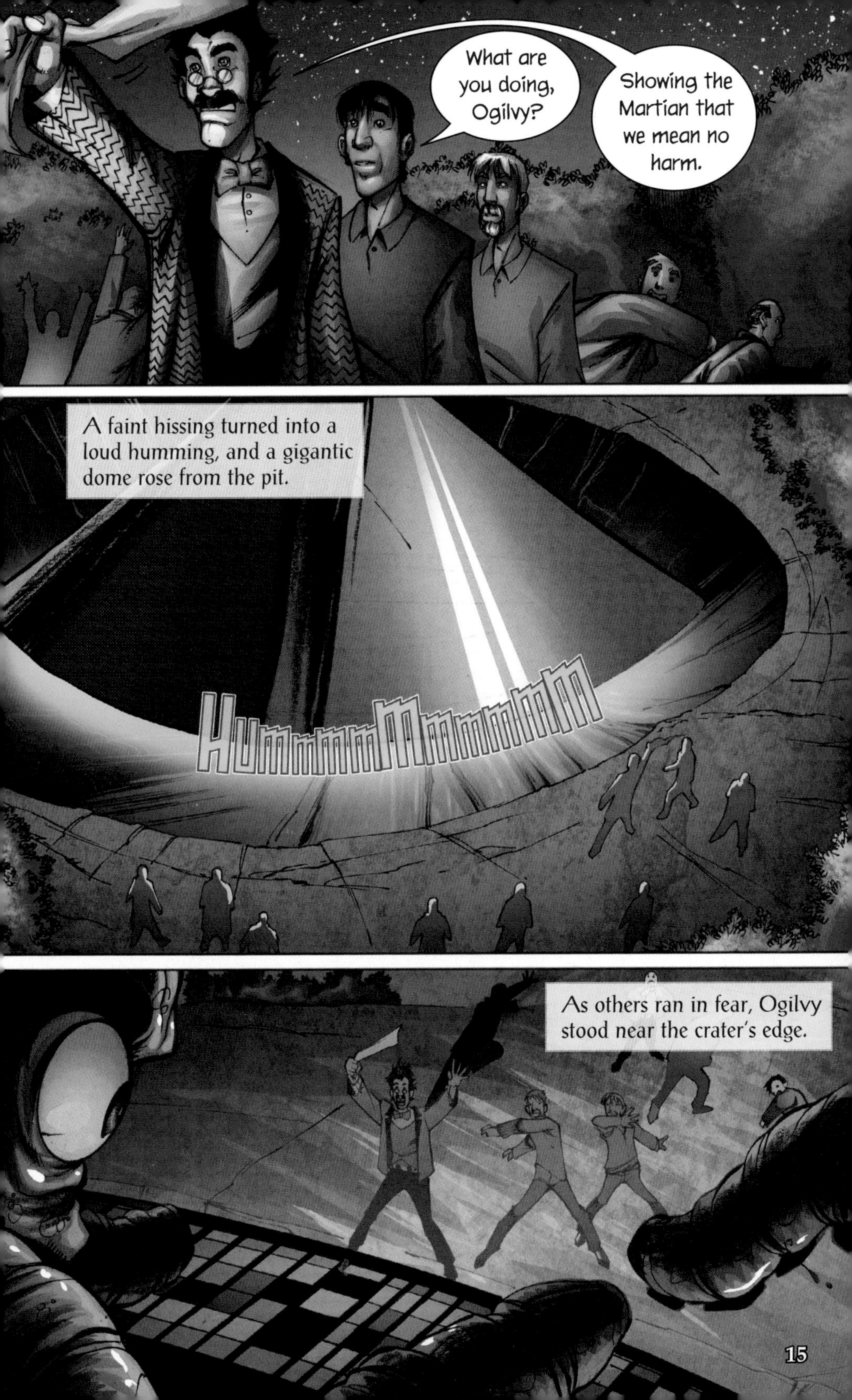
What are you doing, Ogilvy?
Showing the Martian that we mean no harm.
A faint hissing turned into a loud humming, and a gigantic dome rose from the pit.
HUmmmmMMmmmmmM
As others ran in fear, Ogilvy stood near the crater's edge.

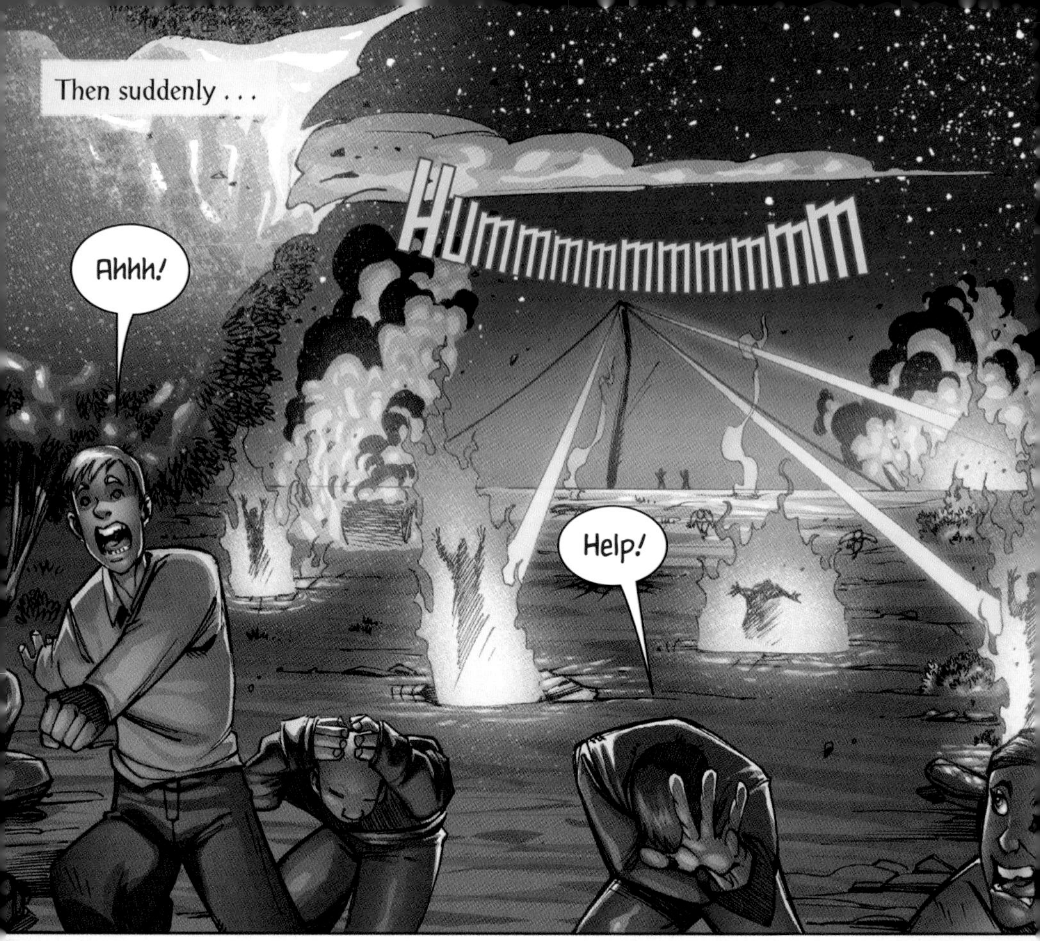
Then suddenly . . .
HUMMMMMMMMMMM
Ahhh!
Help!

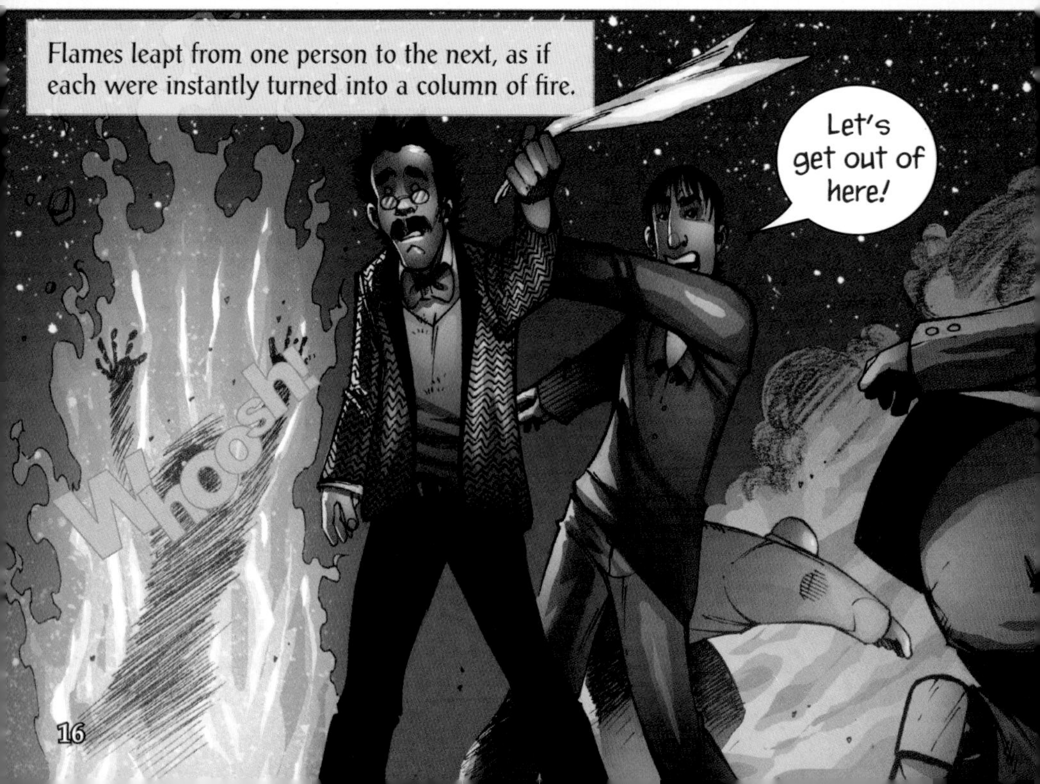
Flames leapt from one person to the next, as if each were instantly turned into a column of fire.
Let's get out of here!
Whoosh!

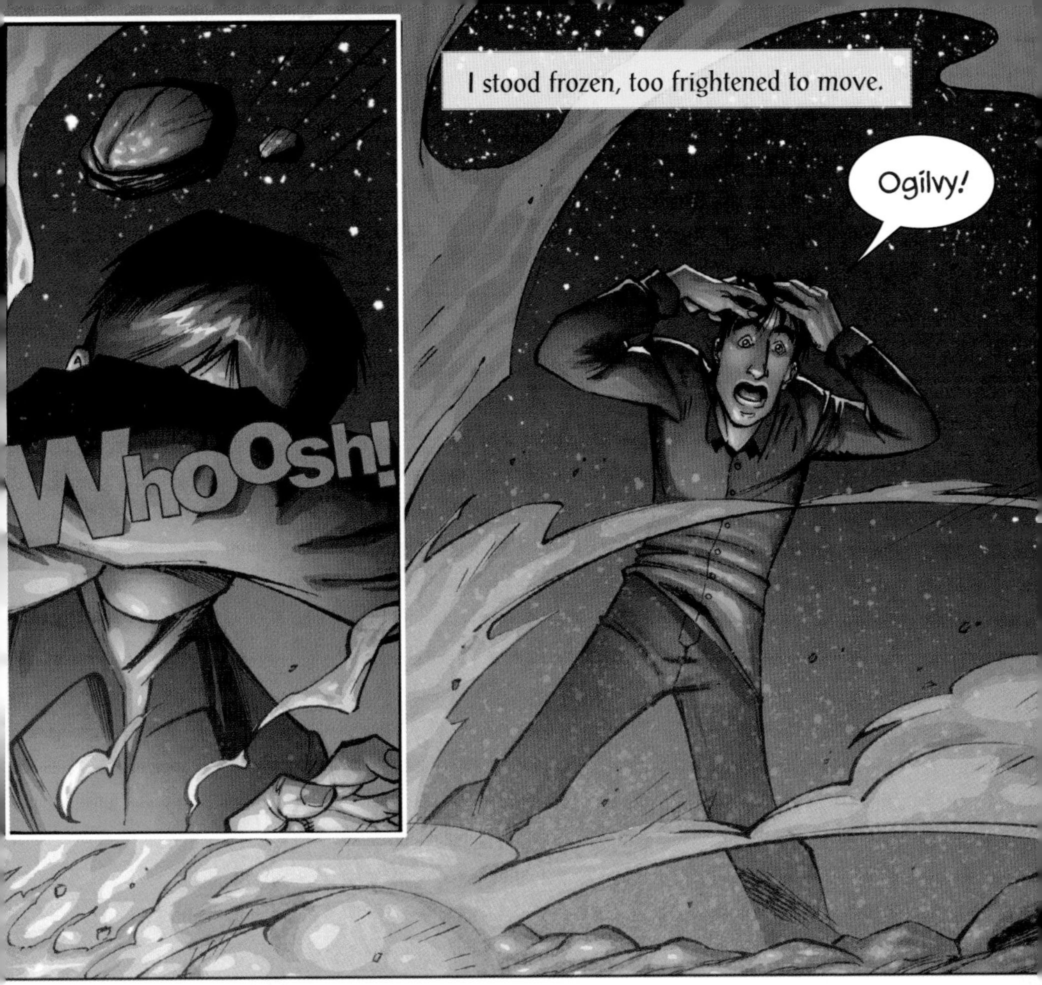
WhoOsh!
I stood frozen, too frightened to move.
Ogilvy!

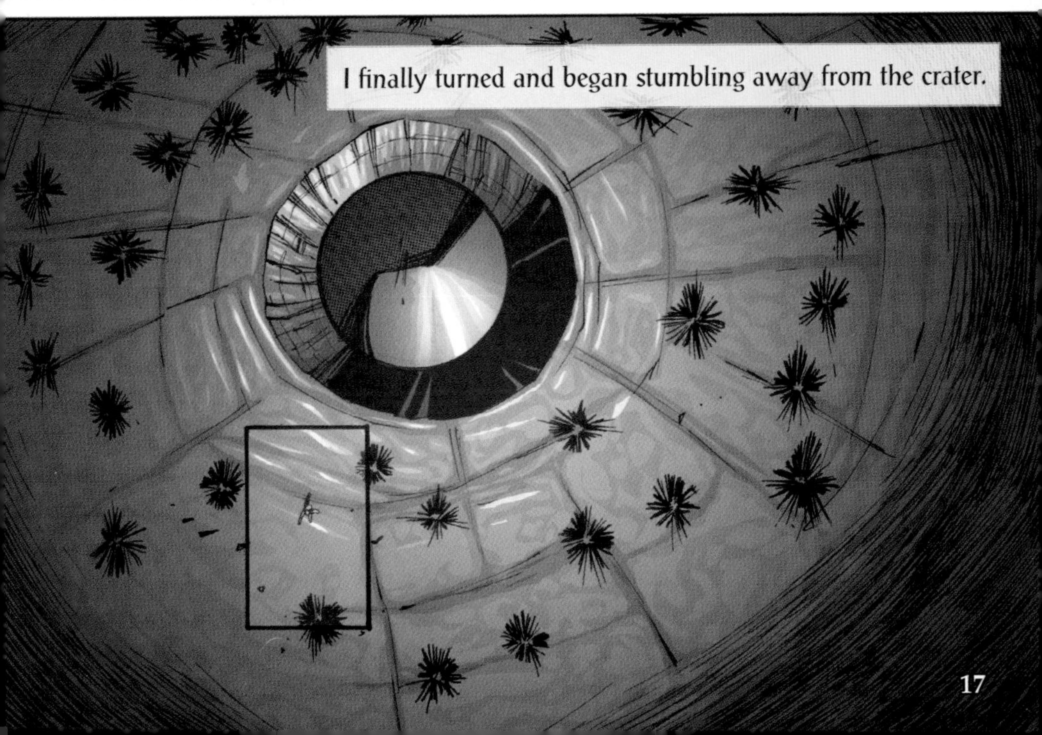
I finally turned and began stumbling away from the crater.

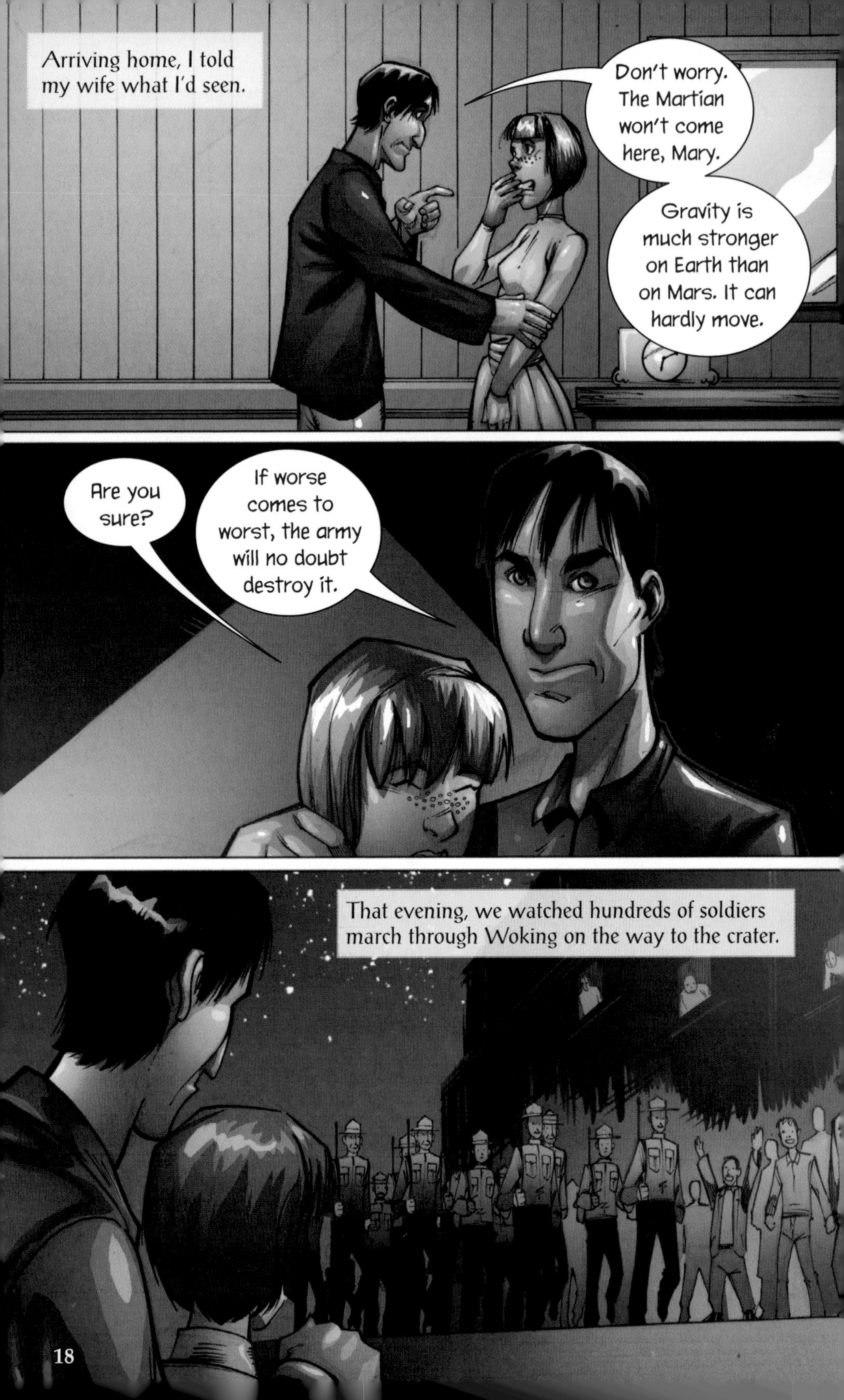
Arriving home, I told my wife what I'd seen.
Don't worry. The Martian won't come here, Mary.
Gravity is much stronger on Earth than on Mars. It can hardly move.
Are you sure?
If worse comes to worst, the army will no doubt destroy it.
That evening, we watched hundreds of soldiers march through Woking on the way to the crater.

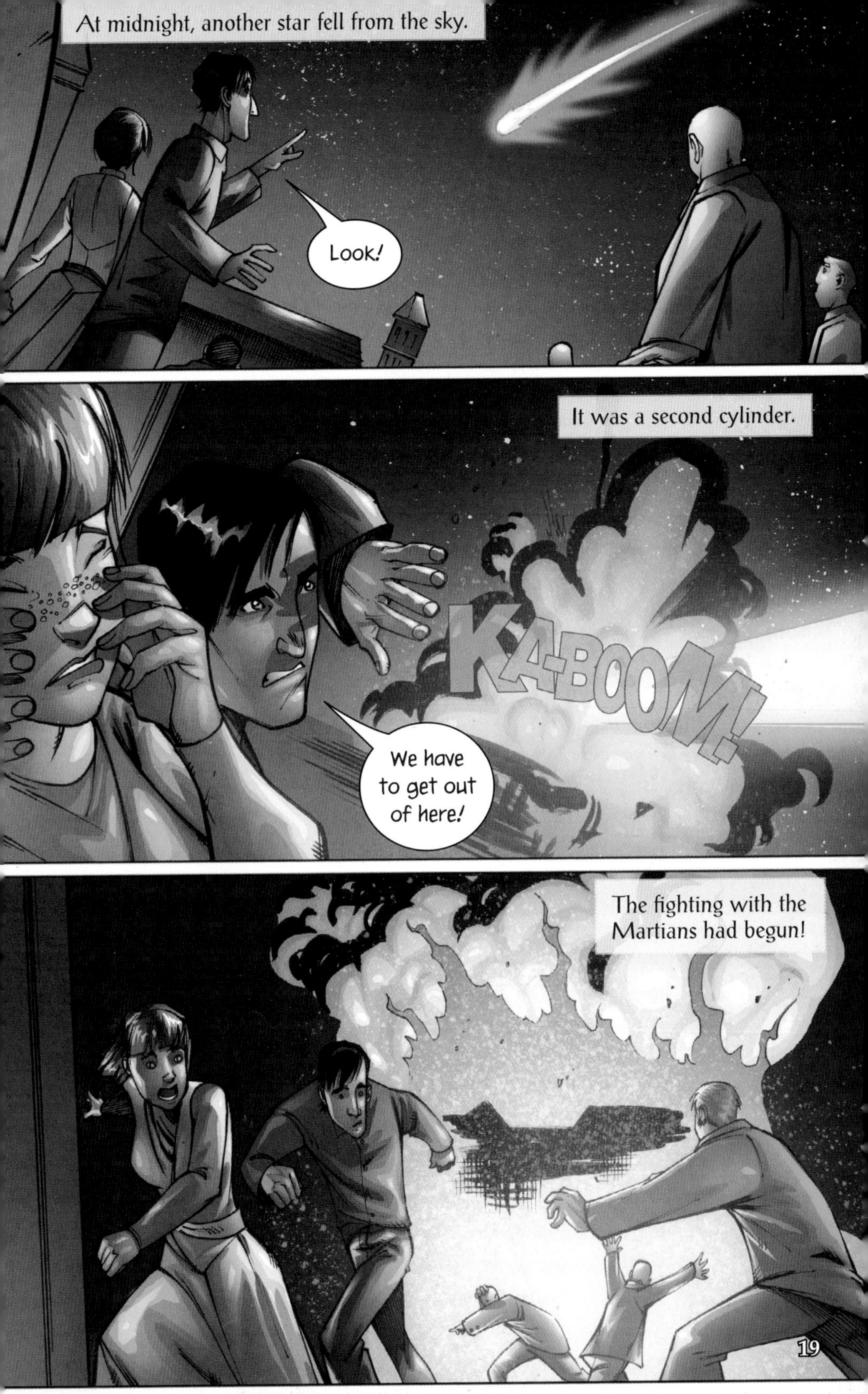
At midnight, another star fell from the sky.
Look!
It was a second cylinder.
KA-BOOM!
We have to get out of here!
The fighting with the Martians had begun!

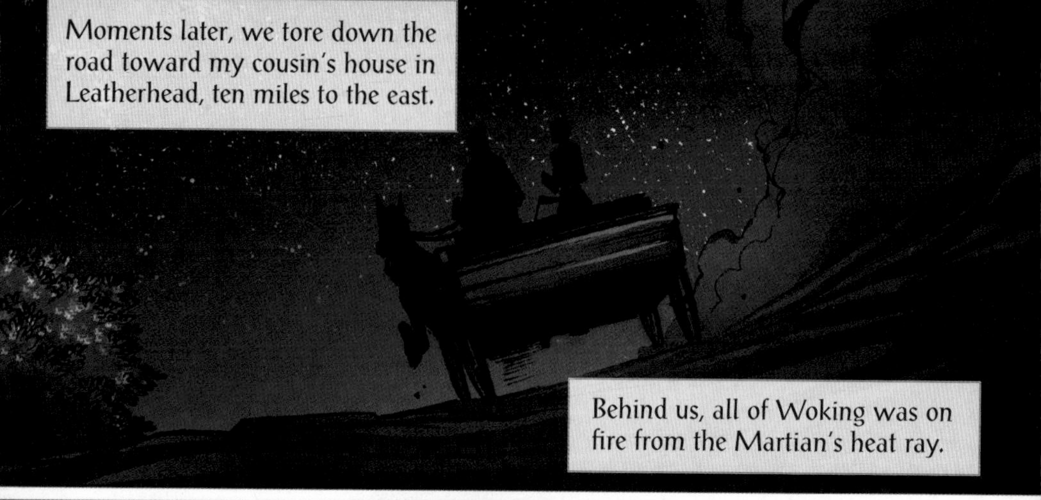
Moments later, we tore down the road toward my cousin's house in Leatherhead, ten miles to the east.
Behind us, all of Woking was on fire from the Martian's heat ray.

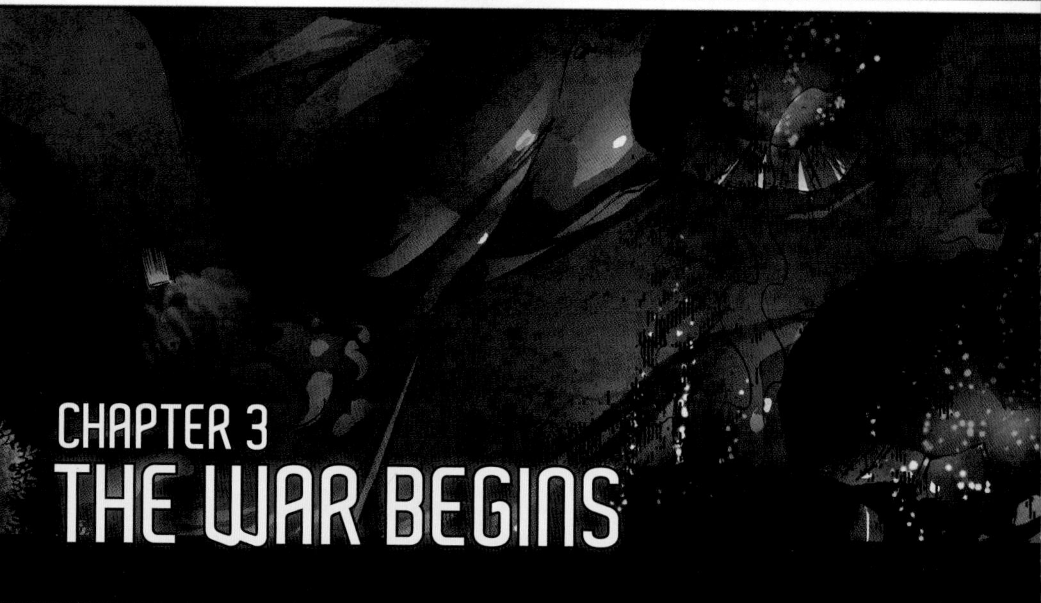

CHAPTER 3
THE WAR BEGINS

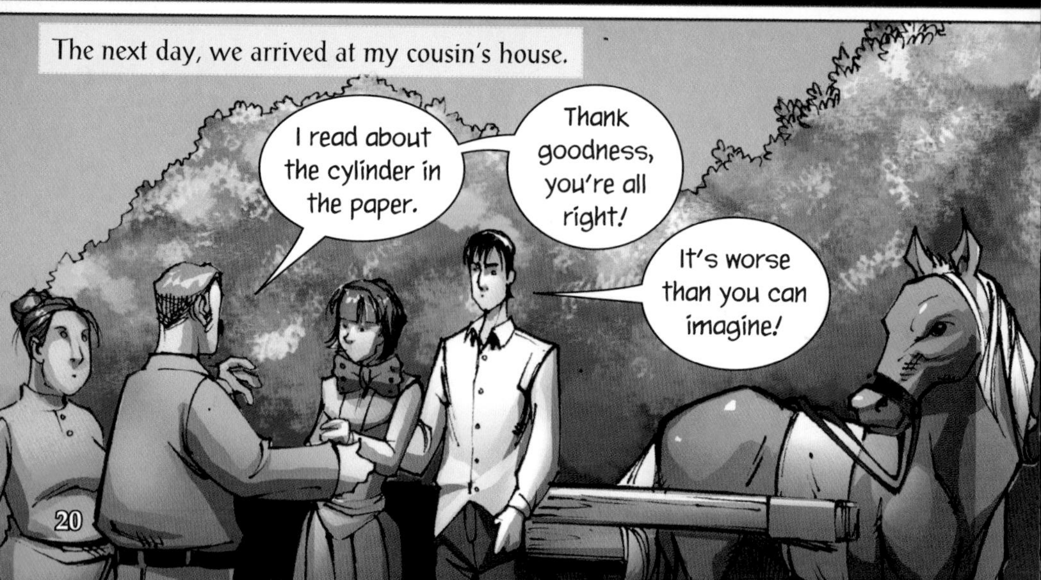
The next day, we arrived at my cousin's house.
I read about the cylinder in the paper.
Thank goodness, you're all right!
It's worse than you can imagine!

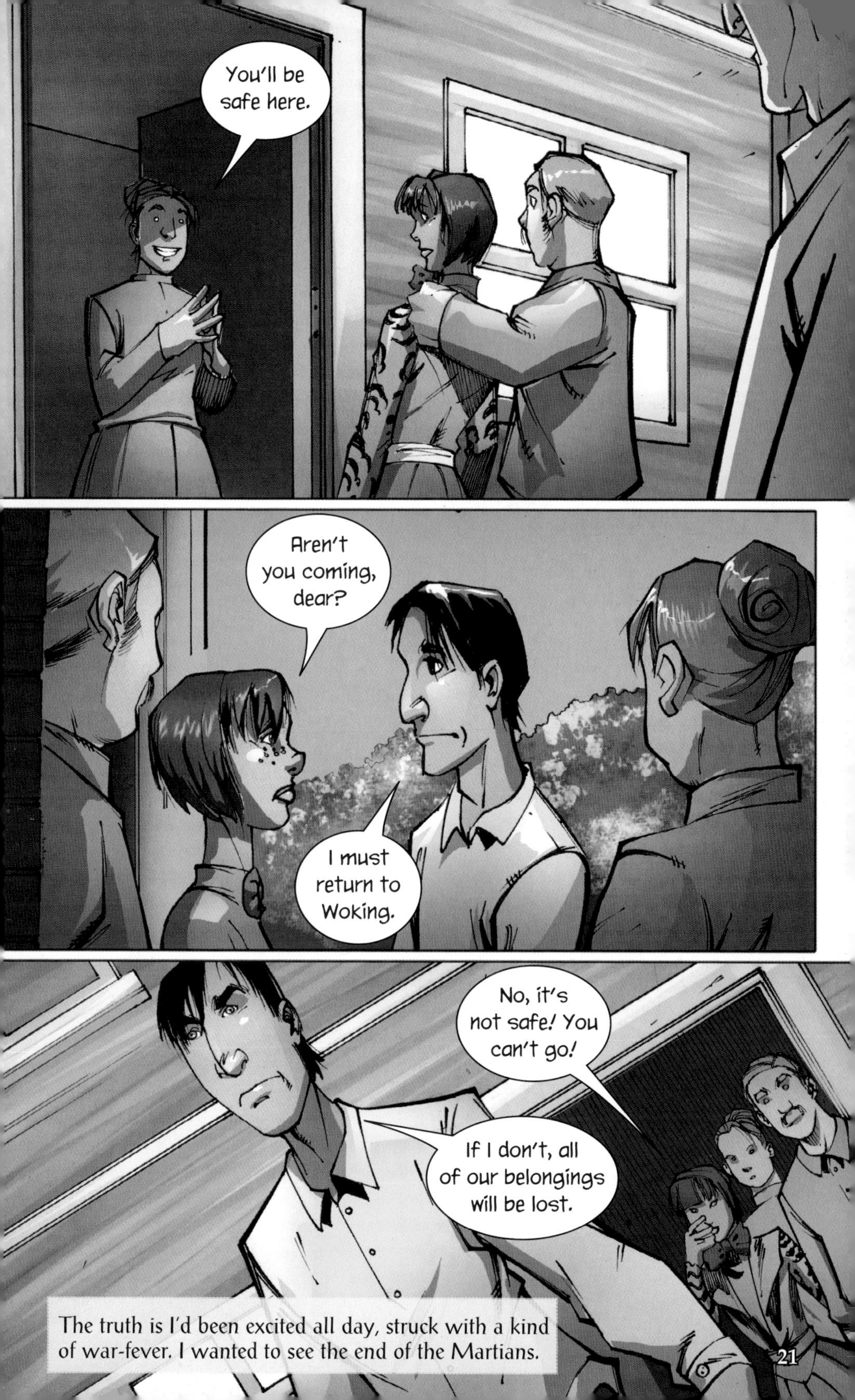
You'll be safe here.
Aren't you coming, dear?
I must return to Woking.
No, it's not safe! You can't go!
If I don't, all of our belongings will be lost.
The truth is I'd been excited all day, struck with a kind of war-fever. I wanted to see the end of the Martians.

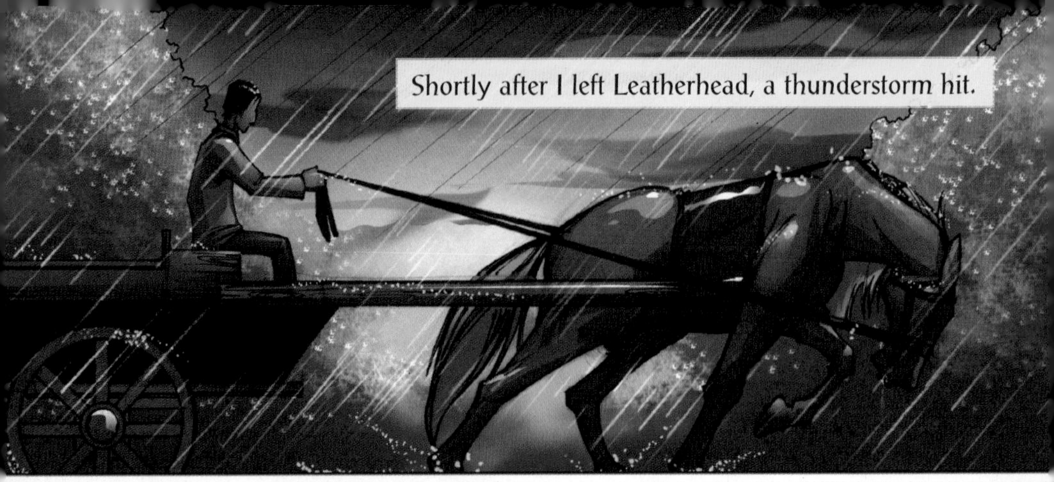
Shortly after I left Leatherhead, a thunderstorm hit.

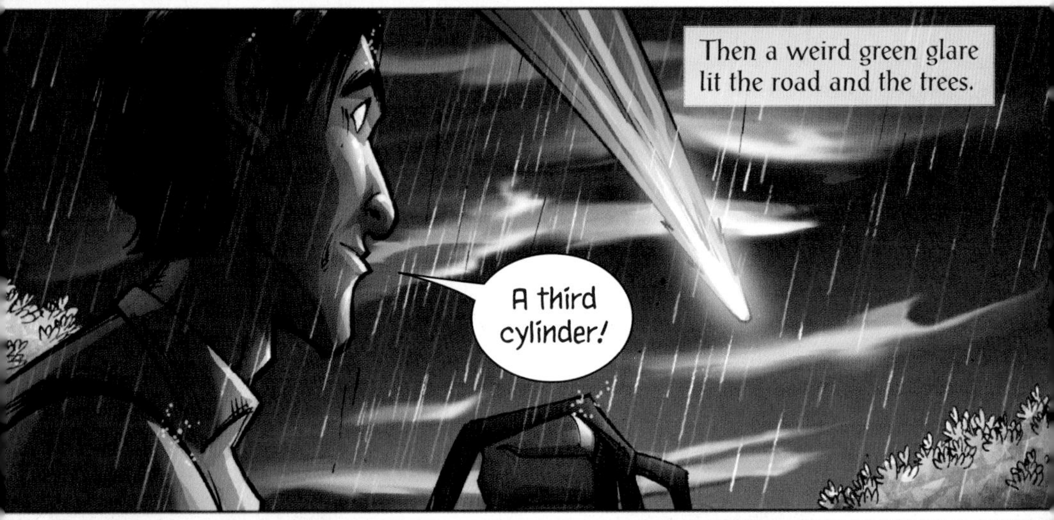
Then a weird green glare lit the road and the trees.
A third cylinder!

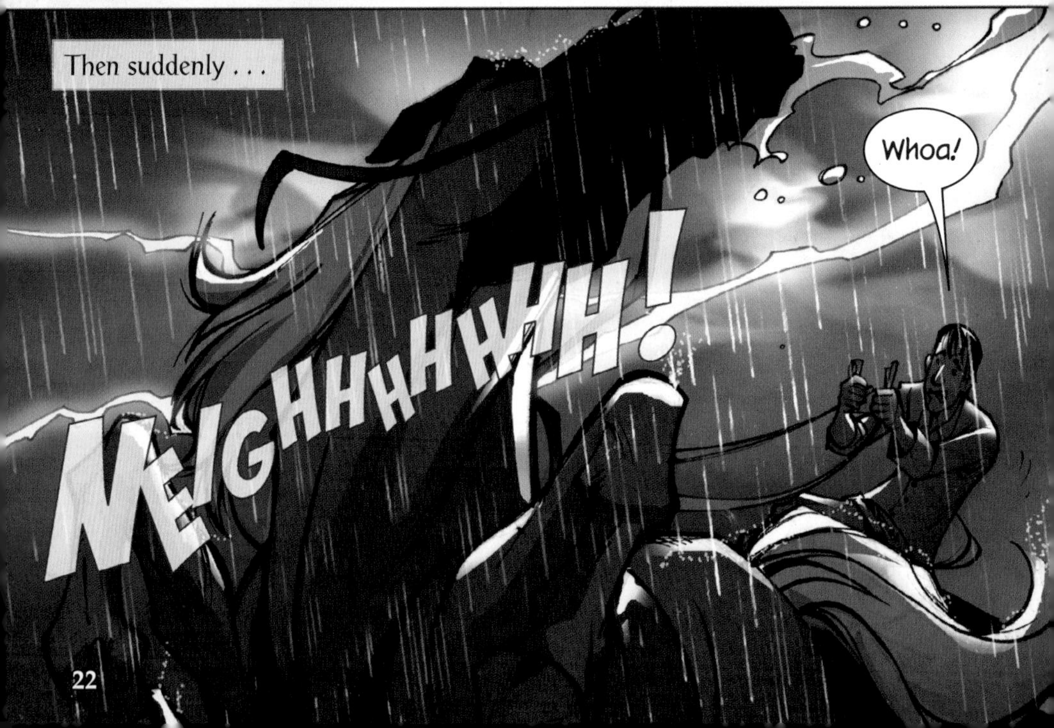
Then suddenly . . .
NEIGHHHHHH!
Whoa!

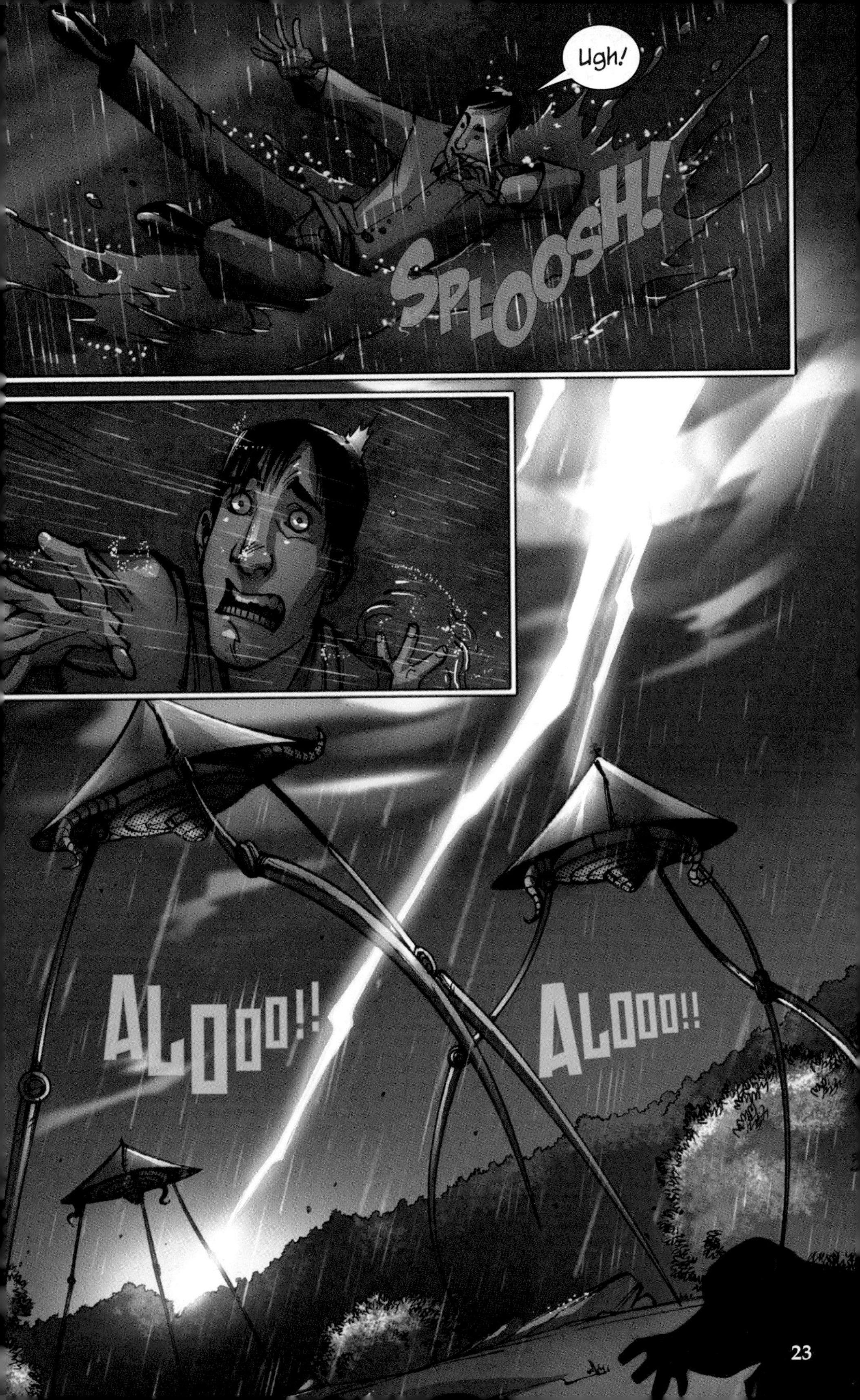
Ugh!
SPLOOSH!
ALOOO!!
ALOOO!!

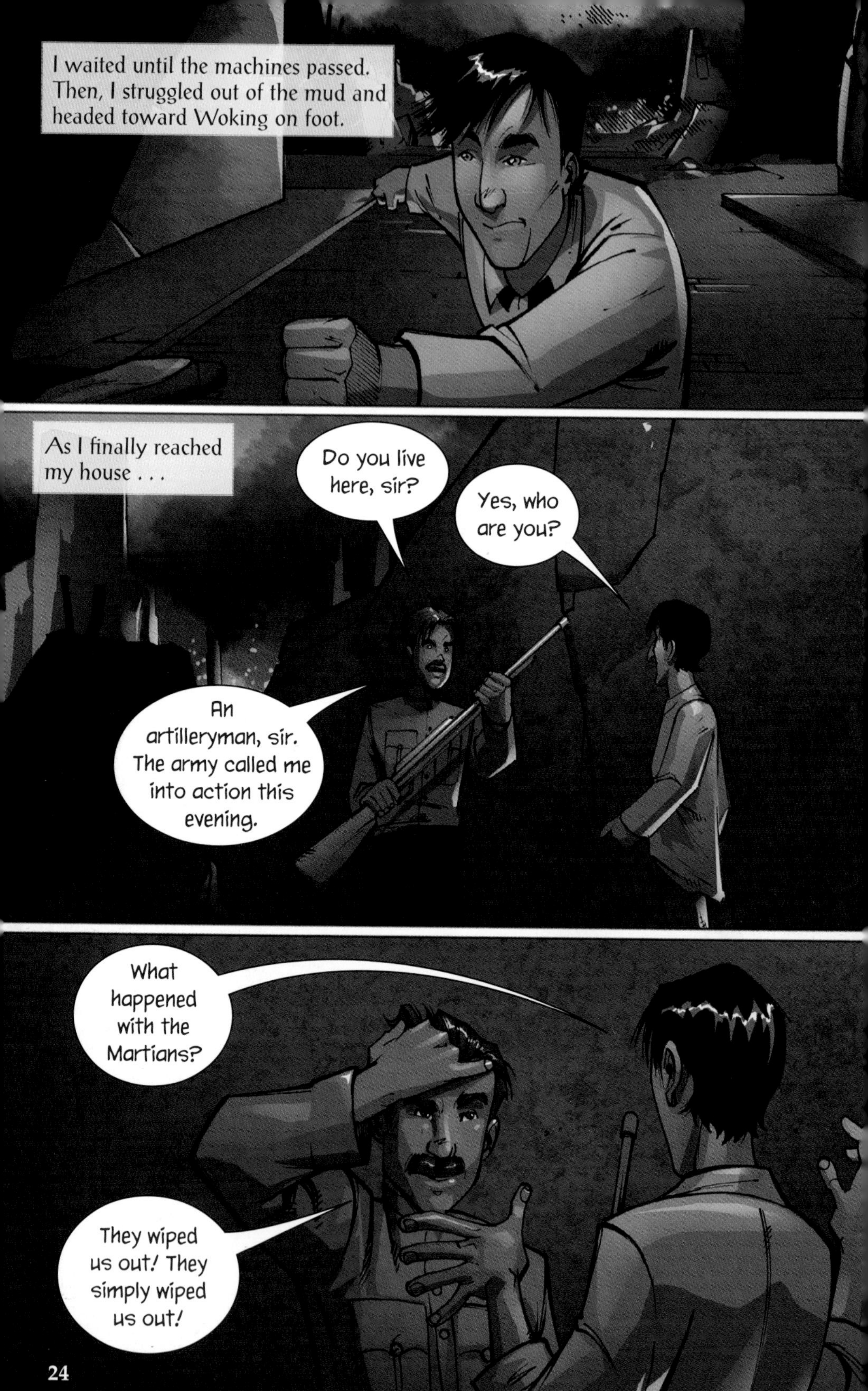
I waited until the machines passed. Then, I struggled out of the mud and headed toward Woking on foot.
As I finally reached my house . . .
Do you live here, sir?
Yes, who are you?
An artilleryman, sir. The army called me into action this evening.
What happened with the Martians?
They wiped us out! They simply wiped us out!

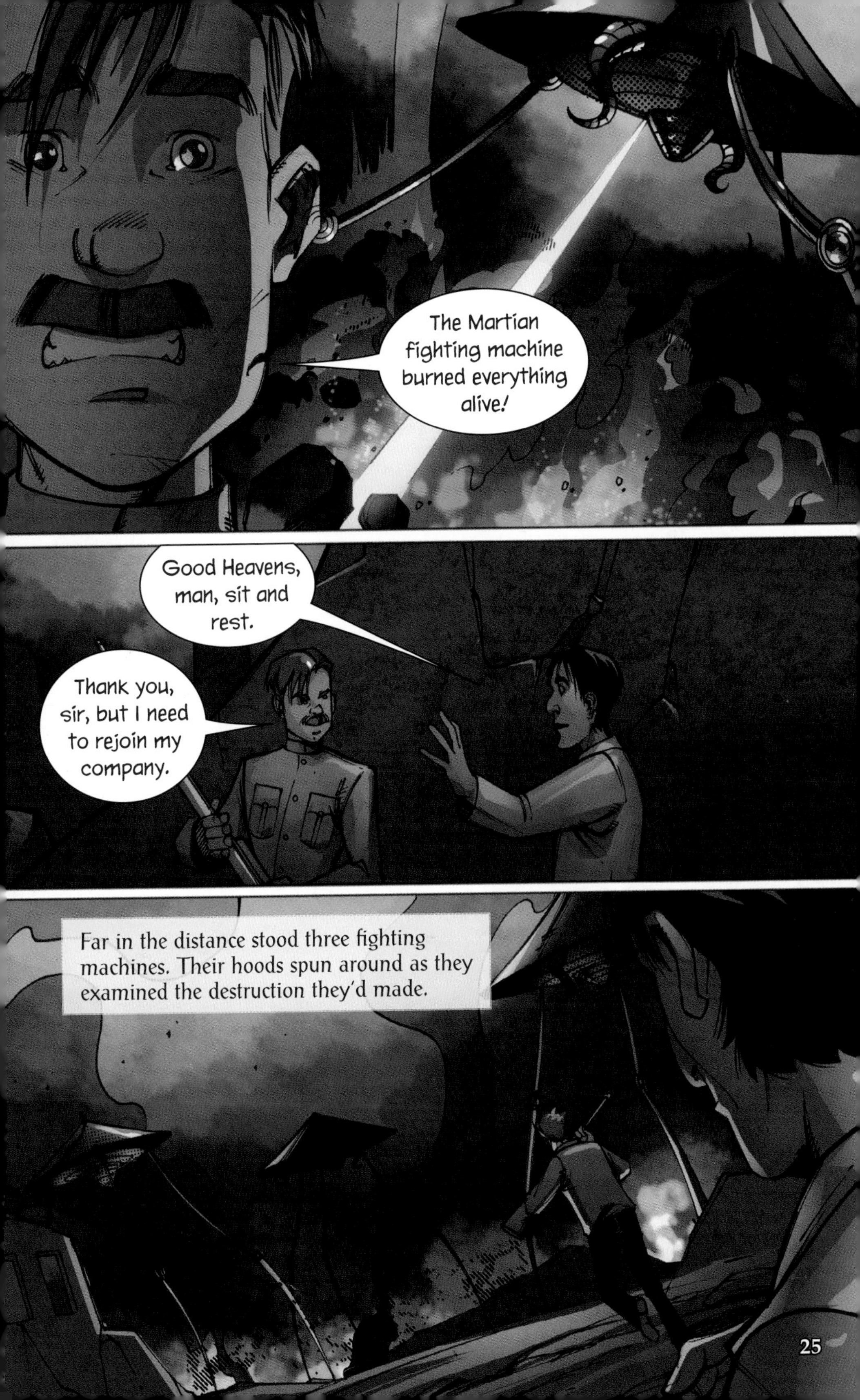
The Martian fighting machine burned everything alive!
Good Heavens, man, sit and rest.
Thank you, sir, but I need to rejoin my company.
Far in the distance stood three fighting machines. Their hoods spun around as they examined the destruction they'd made.

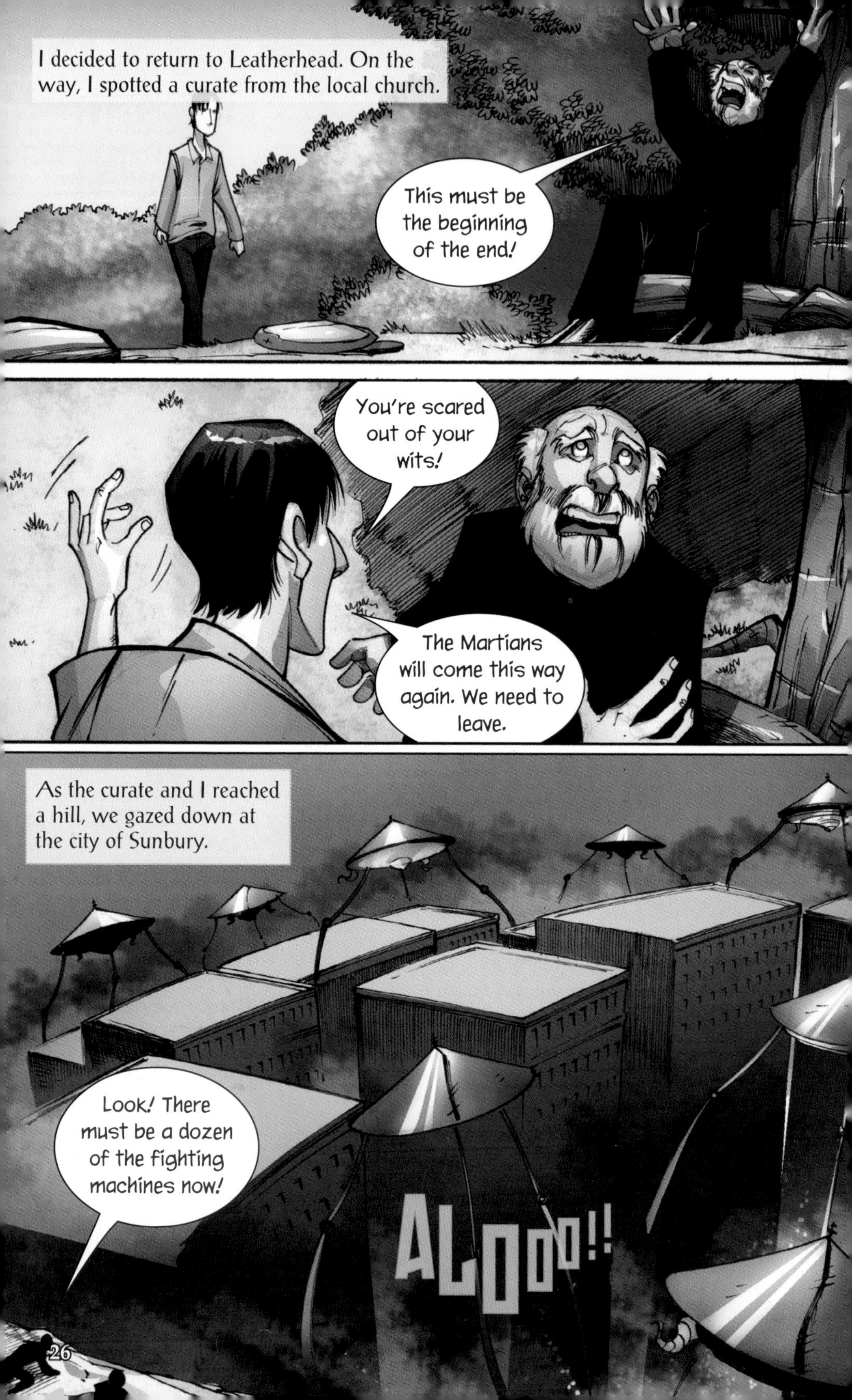

I decided to return to Leatherhead. On the way, I spotted a curate from the local church.
This must be the beginning of the end!
You're scared out of your wits!
The Martians will come this way again. We need to leave.
As the curate and I reached a hill, we gazed down at the city of Sunbury.
Look! There must be a dozen of the fighting machines now!
ALOOO!!

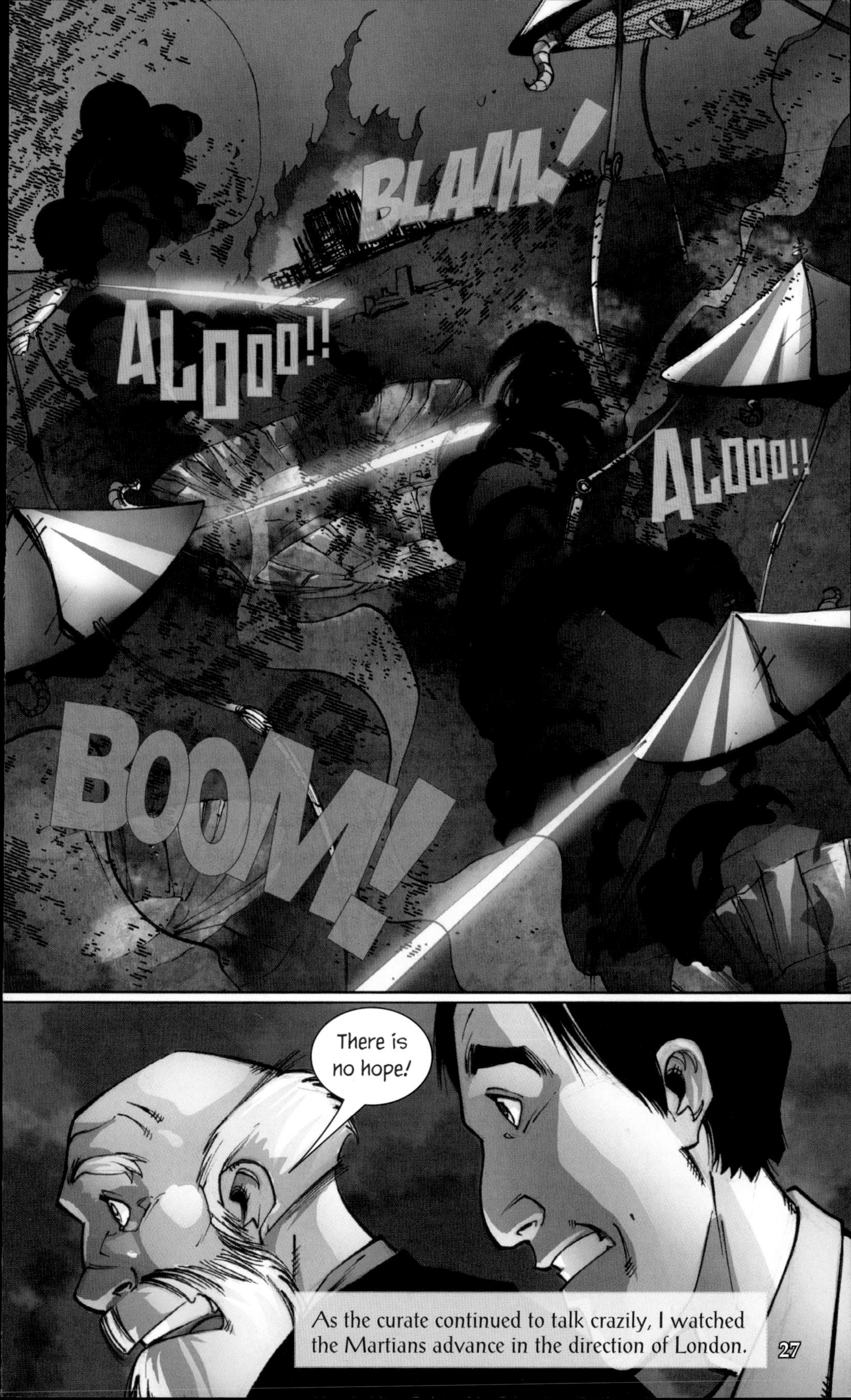
BLAM!
ALOOO!!
ALOOO!!
BOOM!
There is no hope!
As the curate continued to talk crazily, I watched the Martians advance in the direction of London.

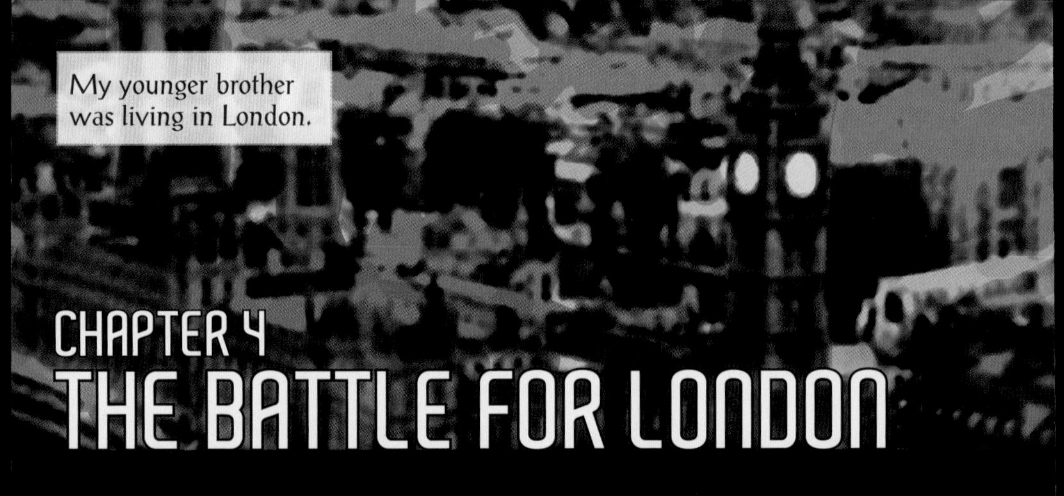
My younger brother was living in London.

CHAPTER 4
THE BATTLE FOR LONDON

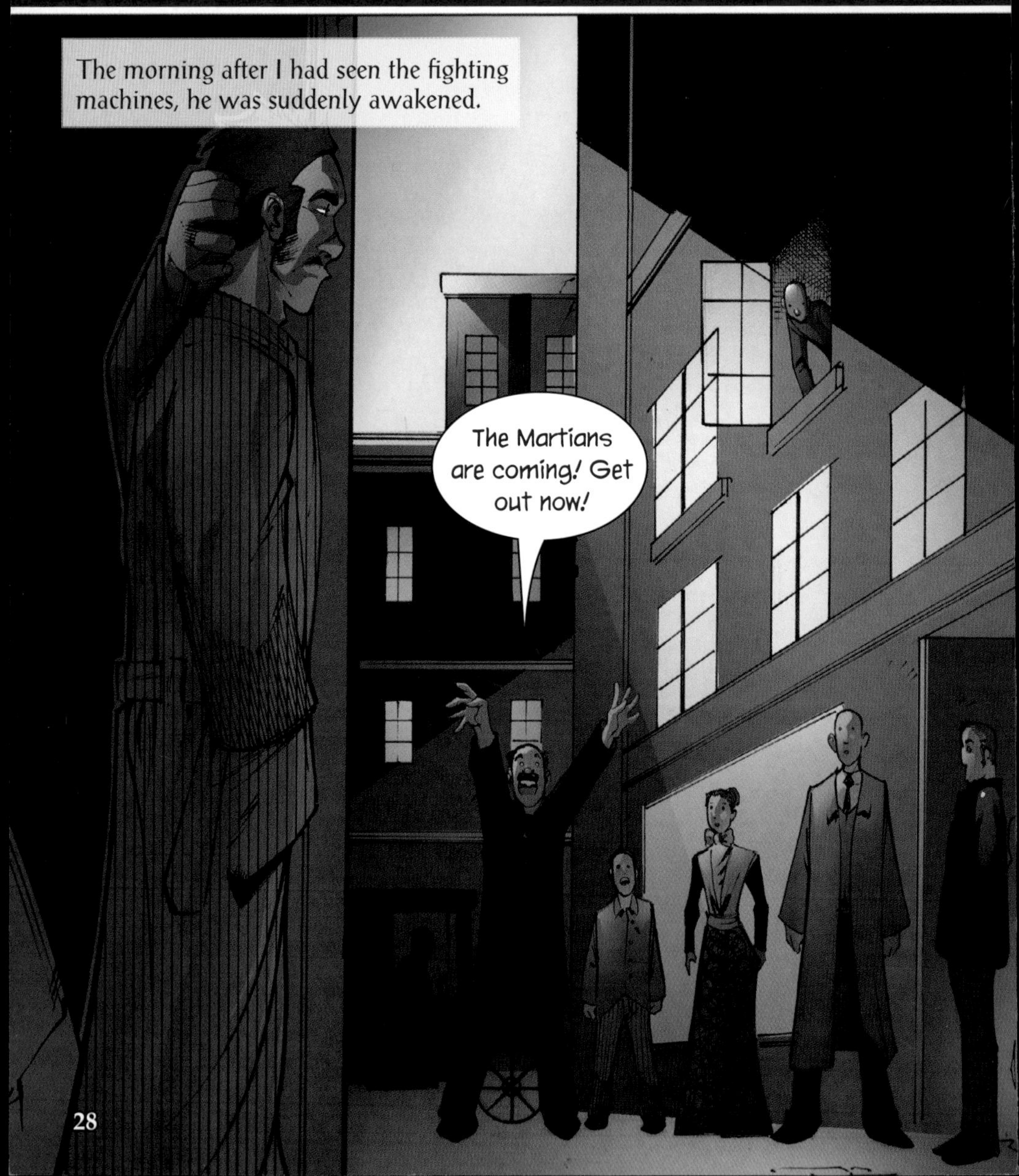
The morning after I had seen the fighting machines, he was suddenly awakened.
The Martians are coming! Get out now!

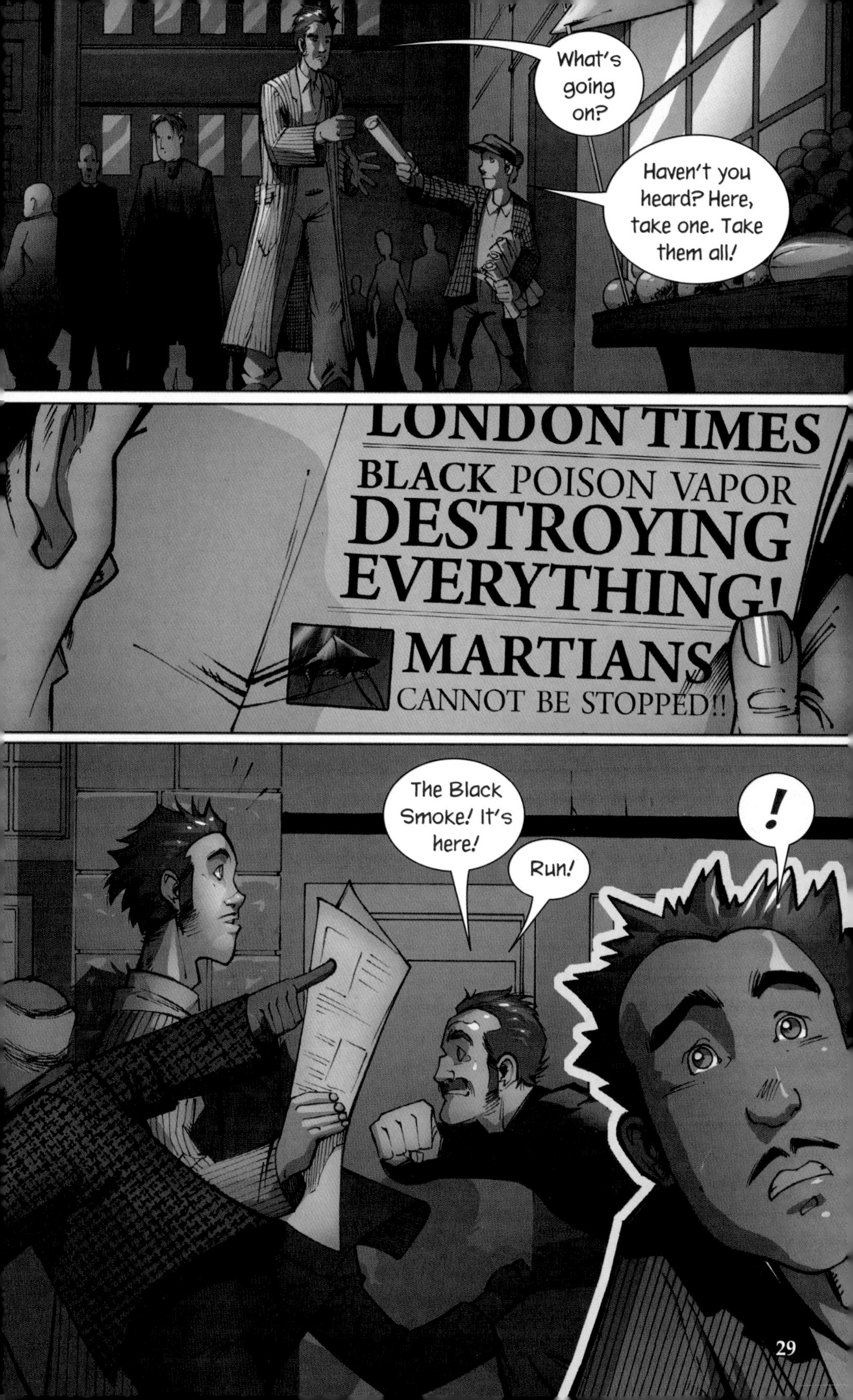
What's going on?
Haven't you heard? Here, take one. Take them all!
LONDON TIMES
BLACK POISON VAPOR
DESTROYING EVERYTHING!
MARTIANS
CANNOT BE STOPPED!!
The Black Smoke! It's here!
Run!
!

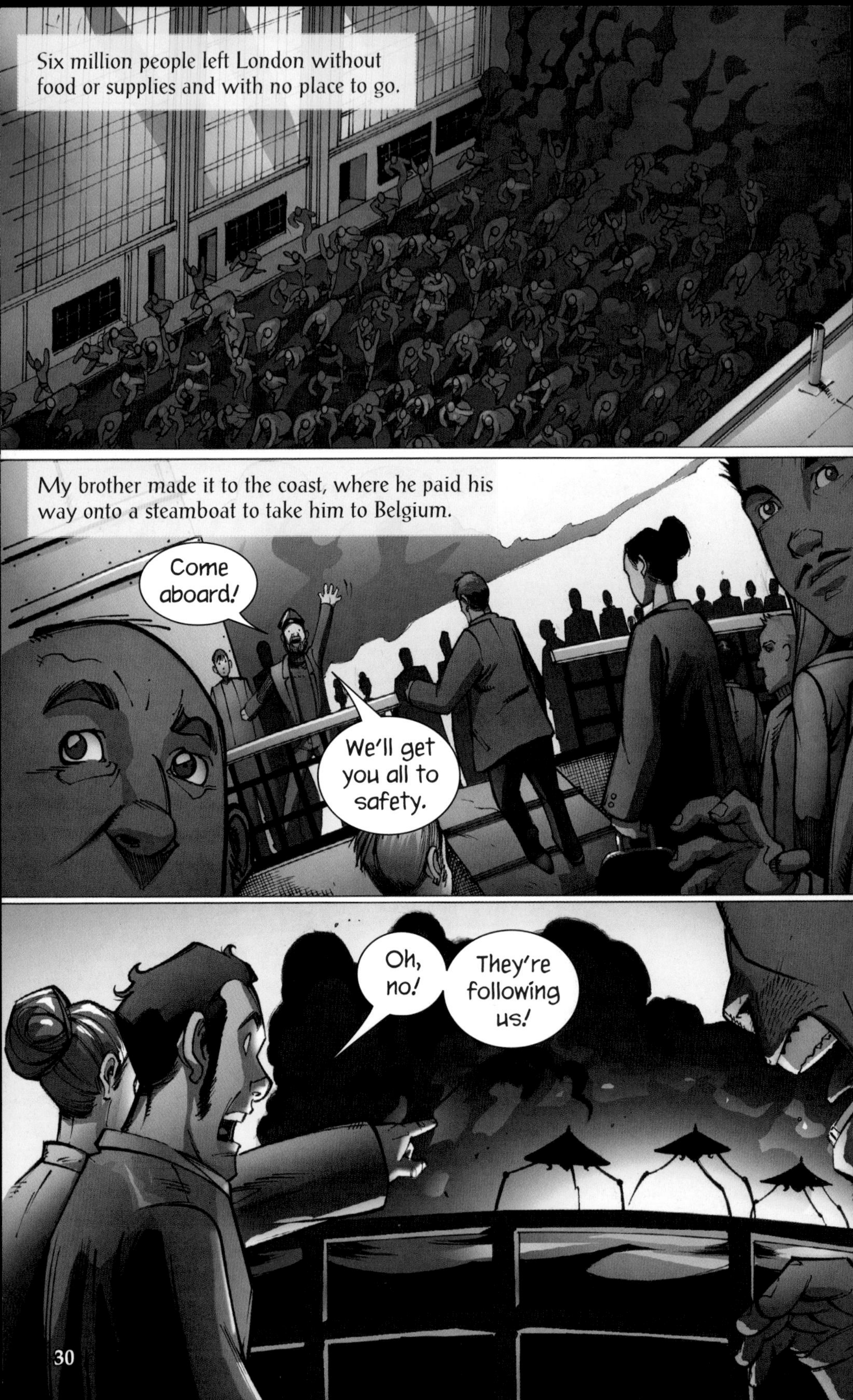
Six million people left London without food or supplies and with no place to go.
My brother made it to the coast, where he paid his way onto a steamboat to take him to Belgium.
Come aboard!
We'll get you all to safety.
Oh, no!
They're following us!

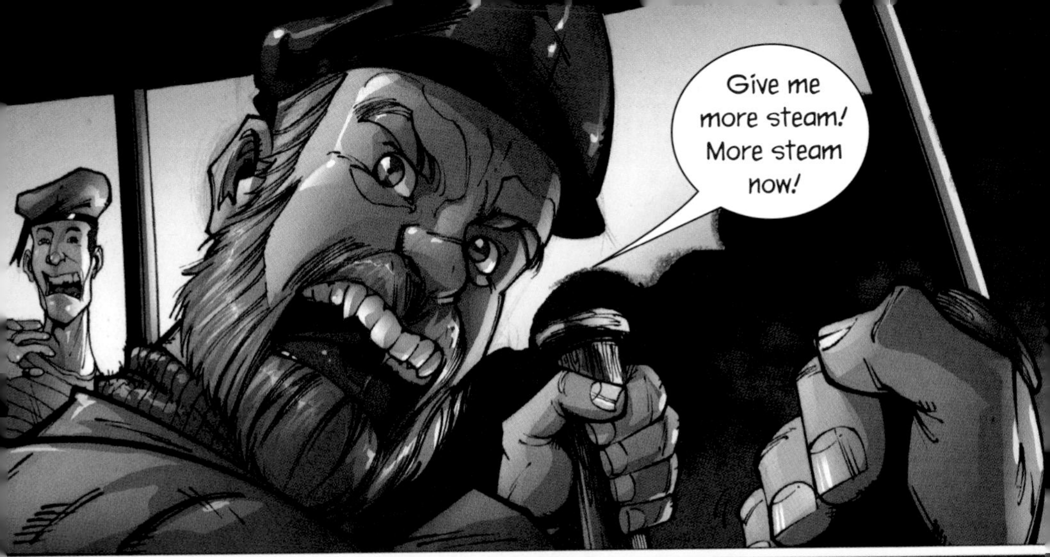
Give me more steam! More steam now!

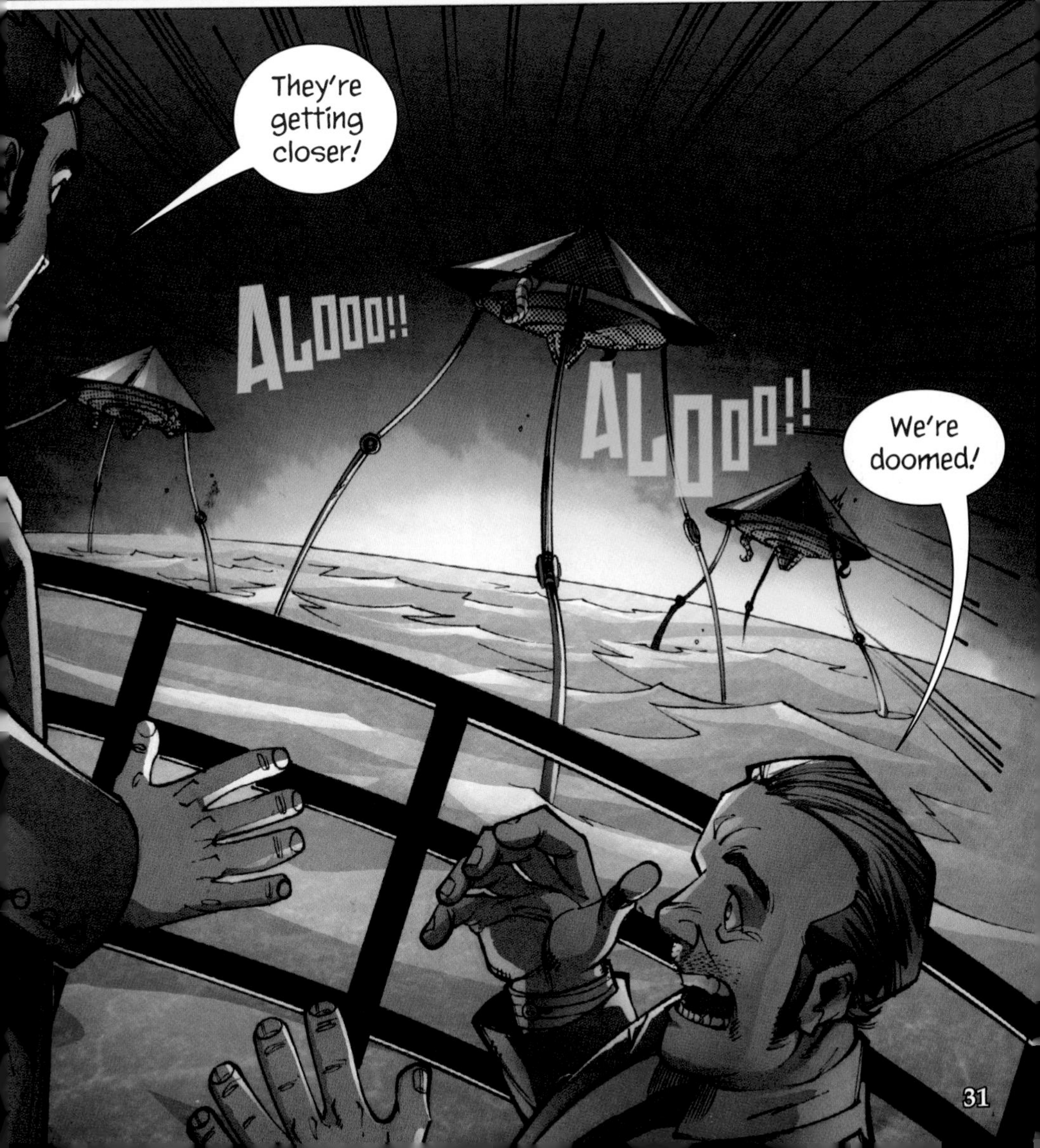
They're getting closer!
ALOOO!!
ALOOO!!
We're doomed!

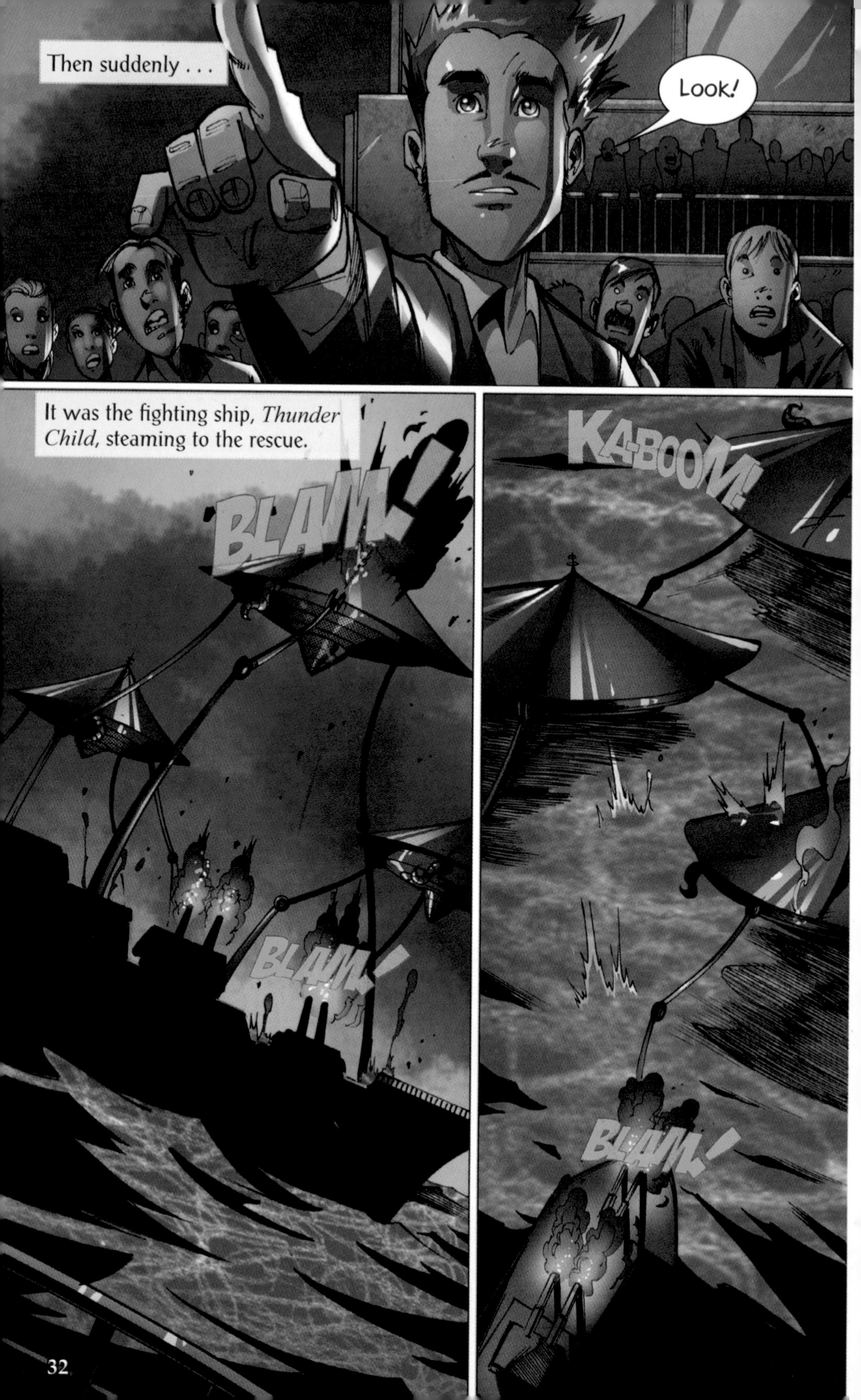
Then suddenly . . .
Look!
It was the fighting ship, *Thunder Child*, steaming to the rescue.
BLAM!
BLAM!
KA-BOOM!
BLAM!

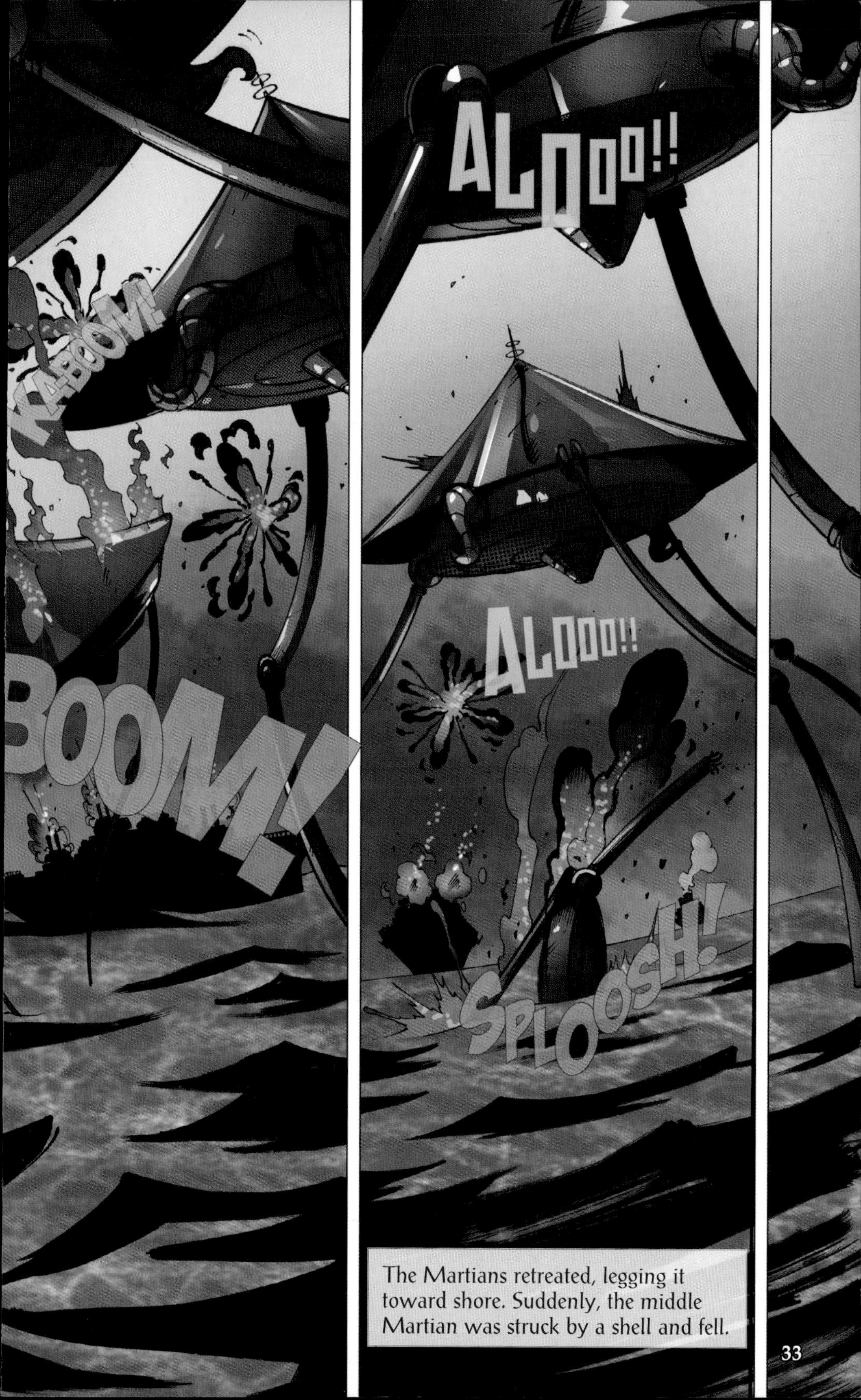
KA-BOOM!
BOOM!
ALOOO!!
ALOOO!!
SPLOOSH!
The Martians retreated, legging it toward shore. Suddenly, the middle Martian was struck by a shell and fell.

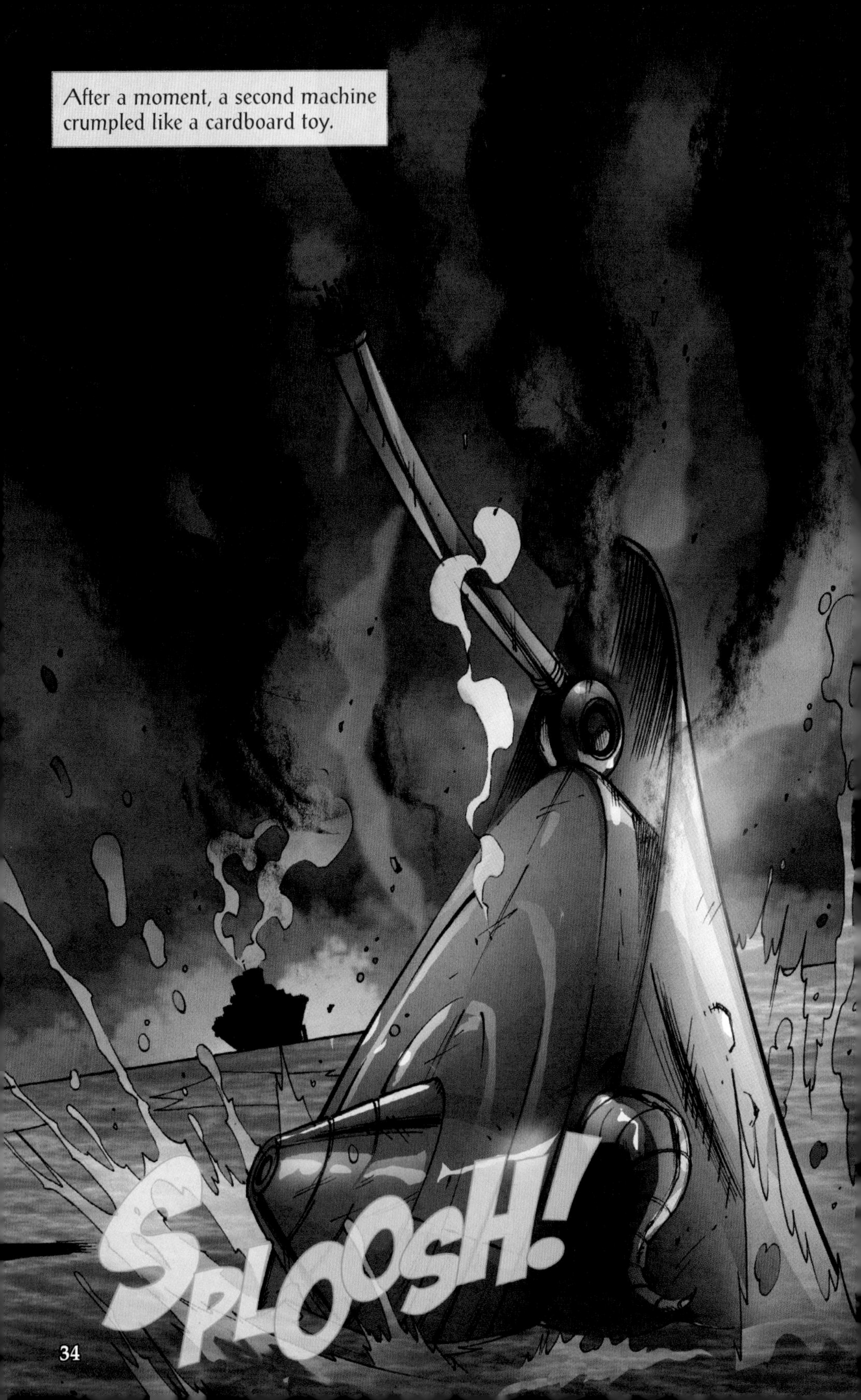
After a moment, a second machine crumpled like a cardboard toy.
SPLOOSH!

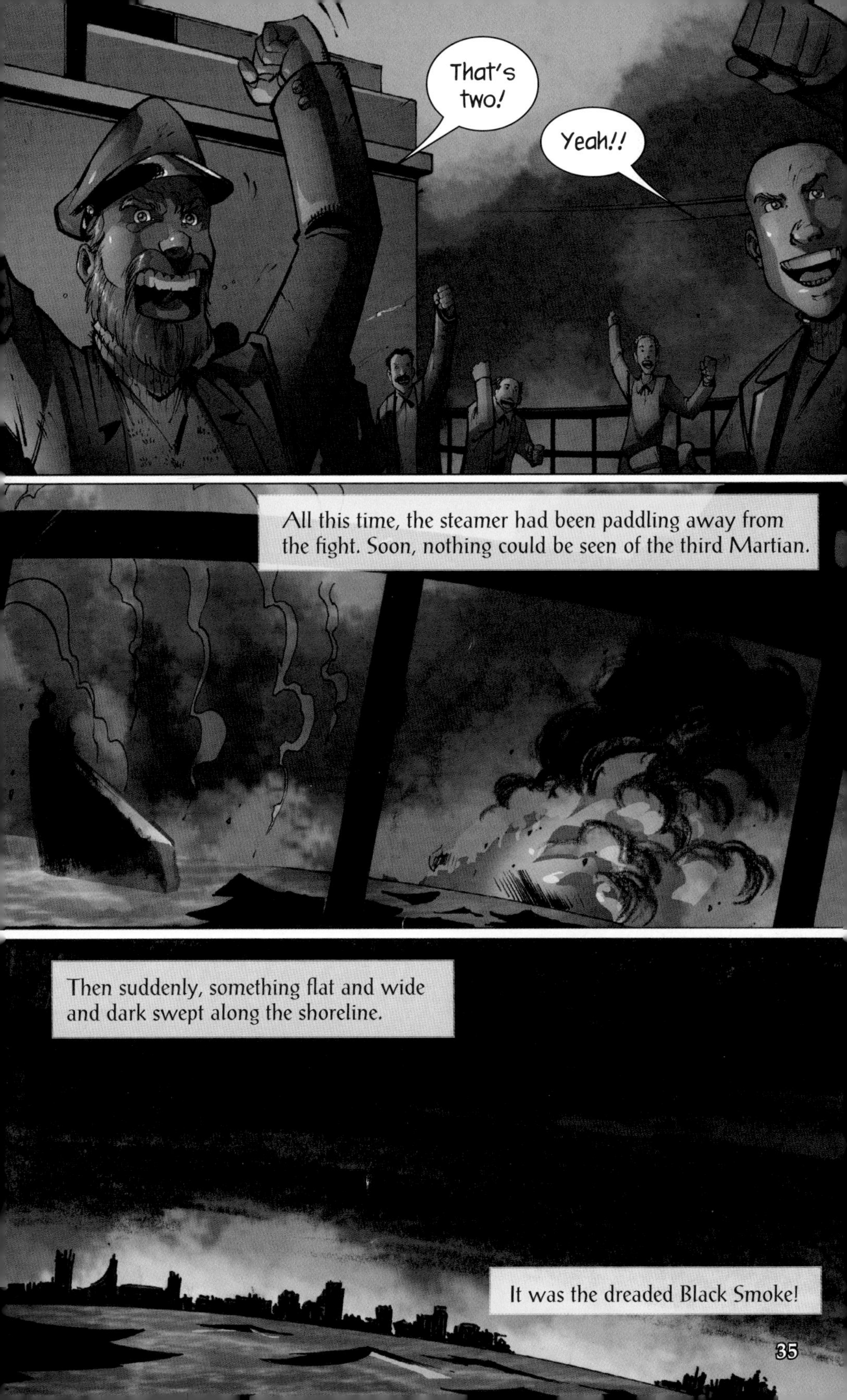
That's two!
Yeah!!
All this time, the steamer had been paddling away from the fight. Soon, nothing could be seen of the third Martian.
Then suddenly, something flat and wide and dark swept along the shoreline.
It was the dreaded Black Smoke!

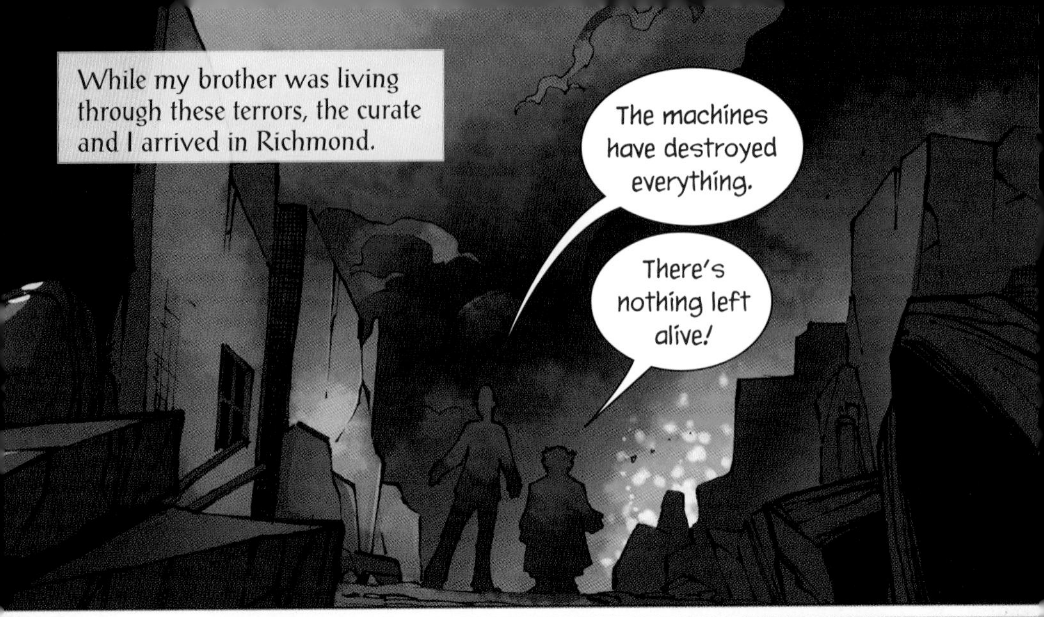
While my brother was living through these terrors, the curate and I arrived in Richmond.
The machines have destroyed everything.
There's nothing left alive!

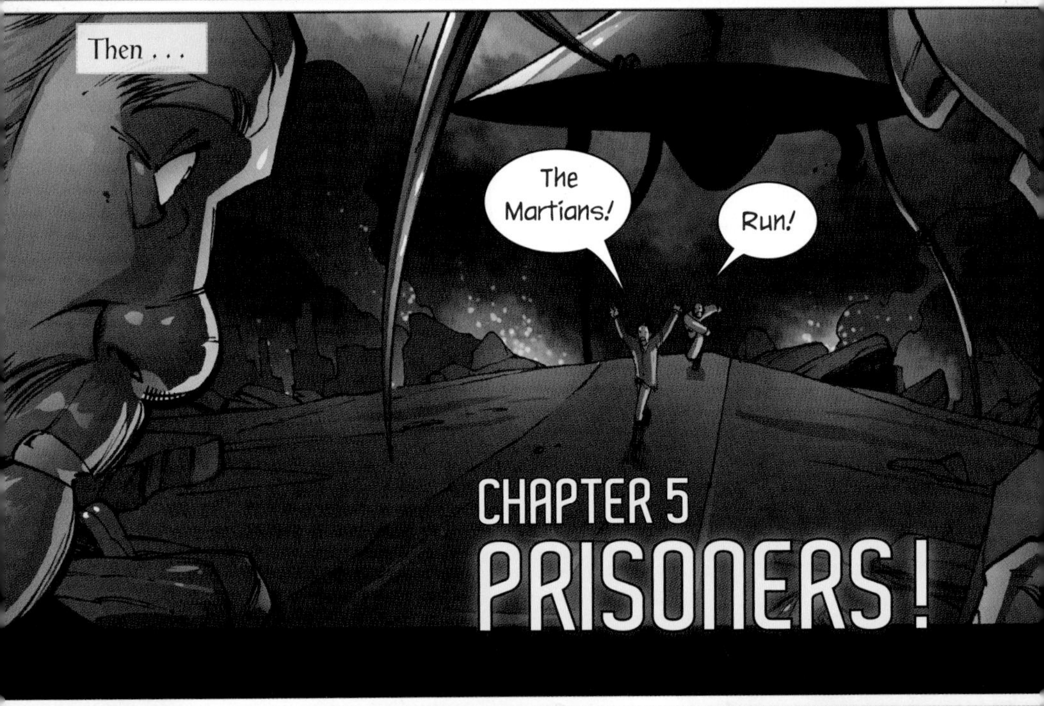
Then . . .
The Martians!
Run!

CHAPTER 5
PRISONERS!

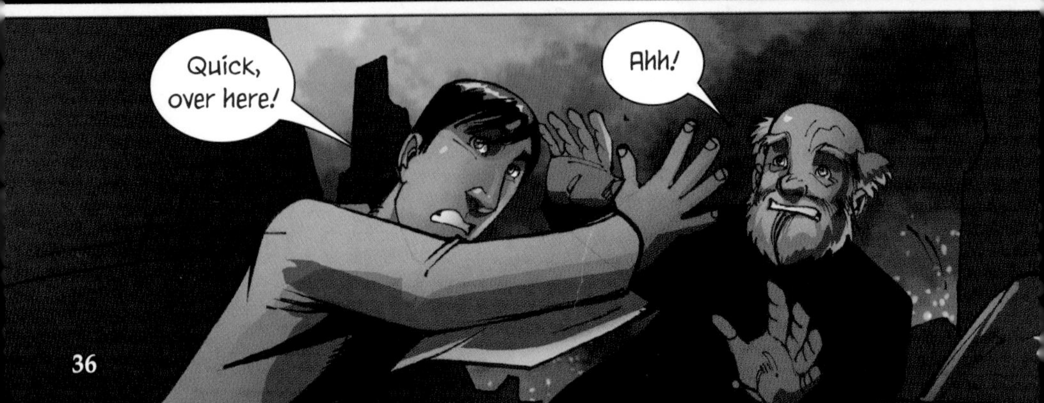
Quick, over here!
Ahh!

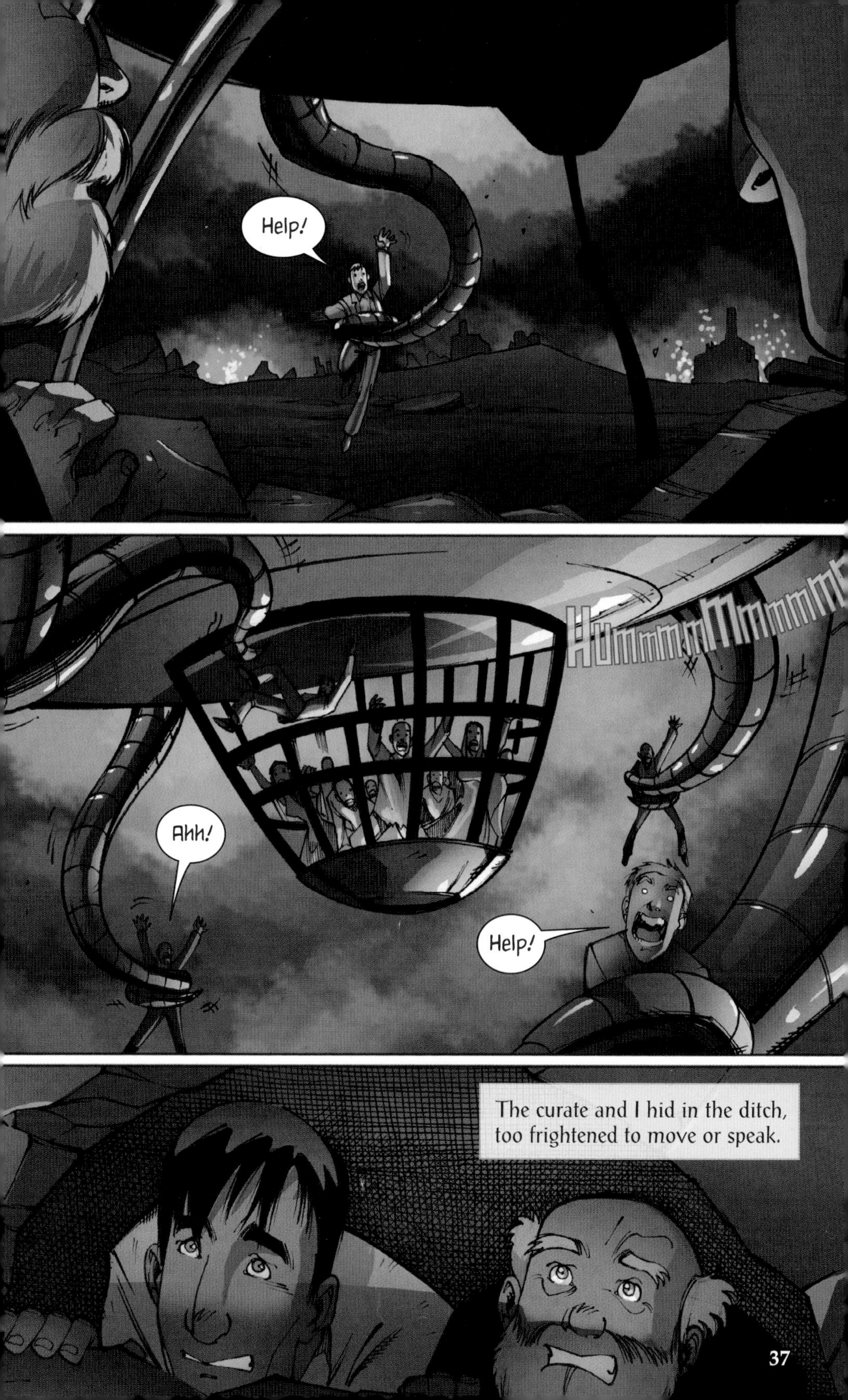
Help!
Ahh!
Help!
The curate and I hid in the ditch, too frightened to move or speak.

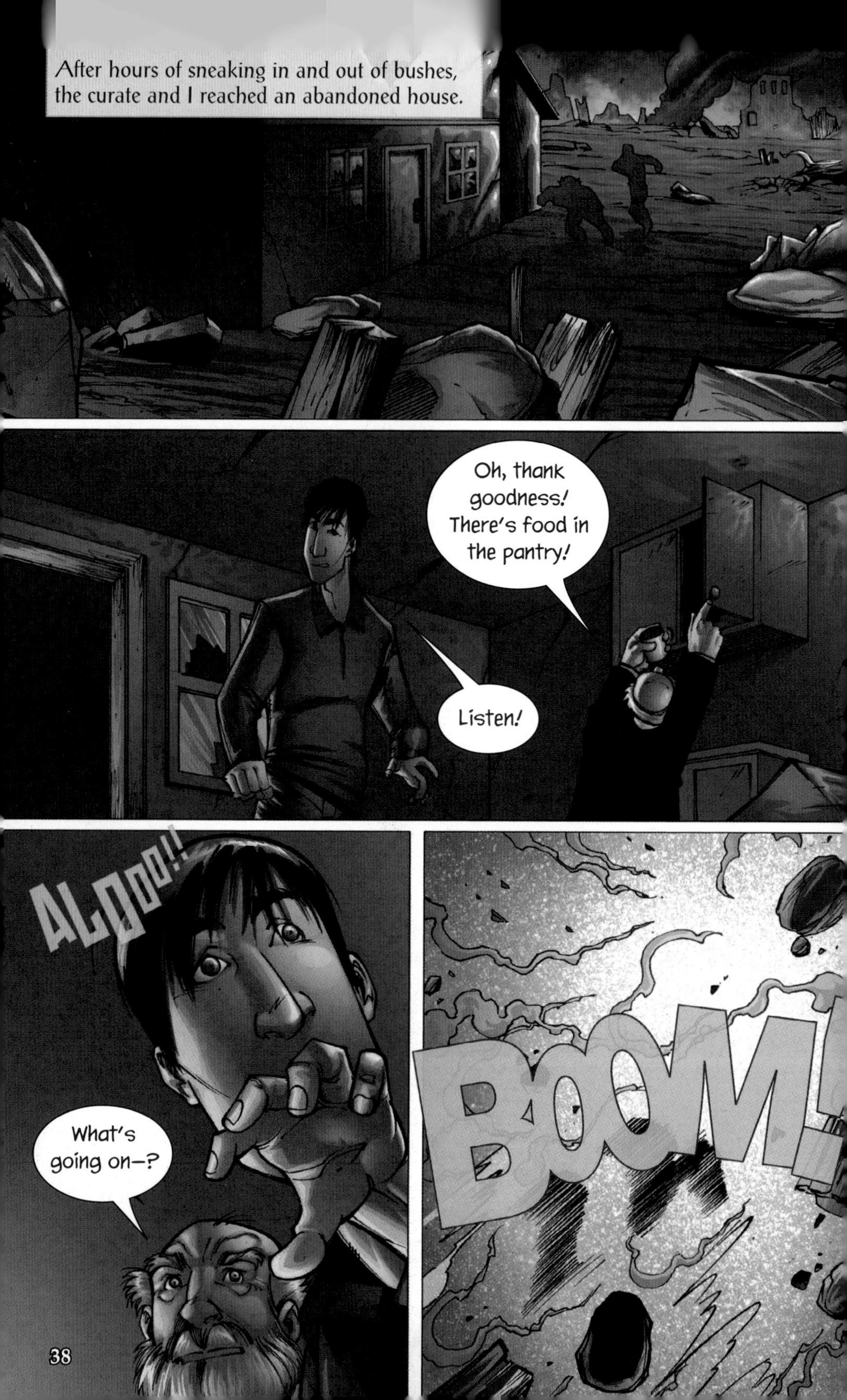
After hours of sneaking in and out of bushes, the curate and I reached an abandoned house.
Oh, thank goodness! There's food in the pantry!
Listen!
ALOOO!!
What's going on–?
BOOM!

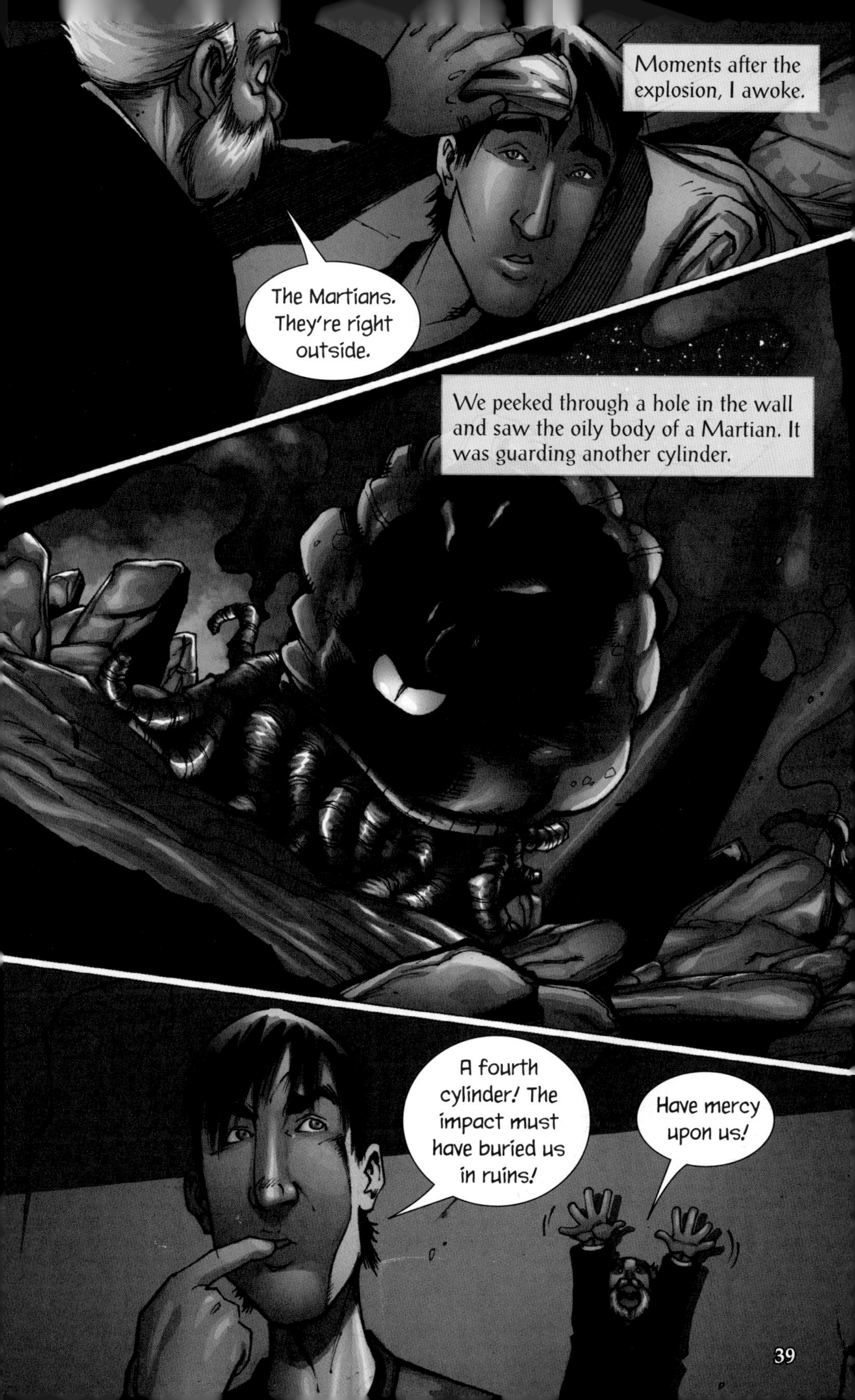

Moments after the explosion, I awoke.
The Martians. They're right outside.
We peeked through a hole in the wall and saw the oily body of a Martian. It was guarding another cylinder.
A fourth cylinder! The impact must have buried us in ruins!
Have mercy upon us!

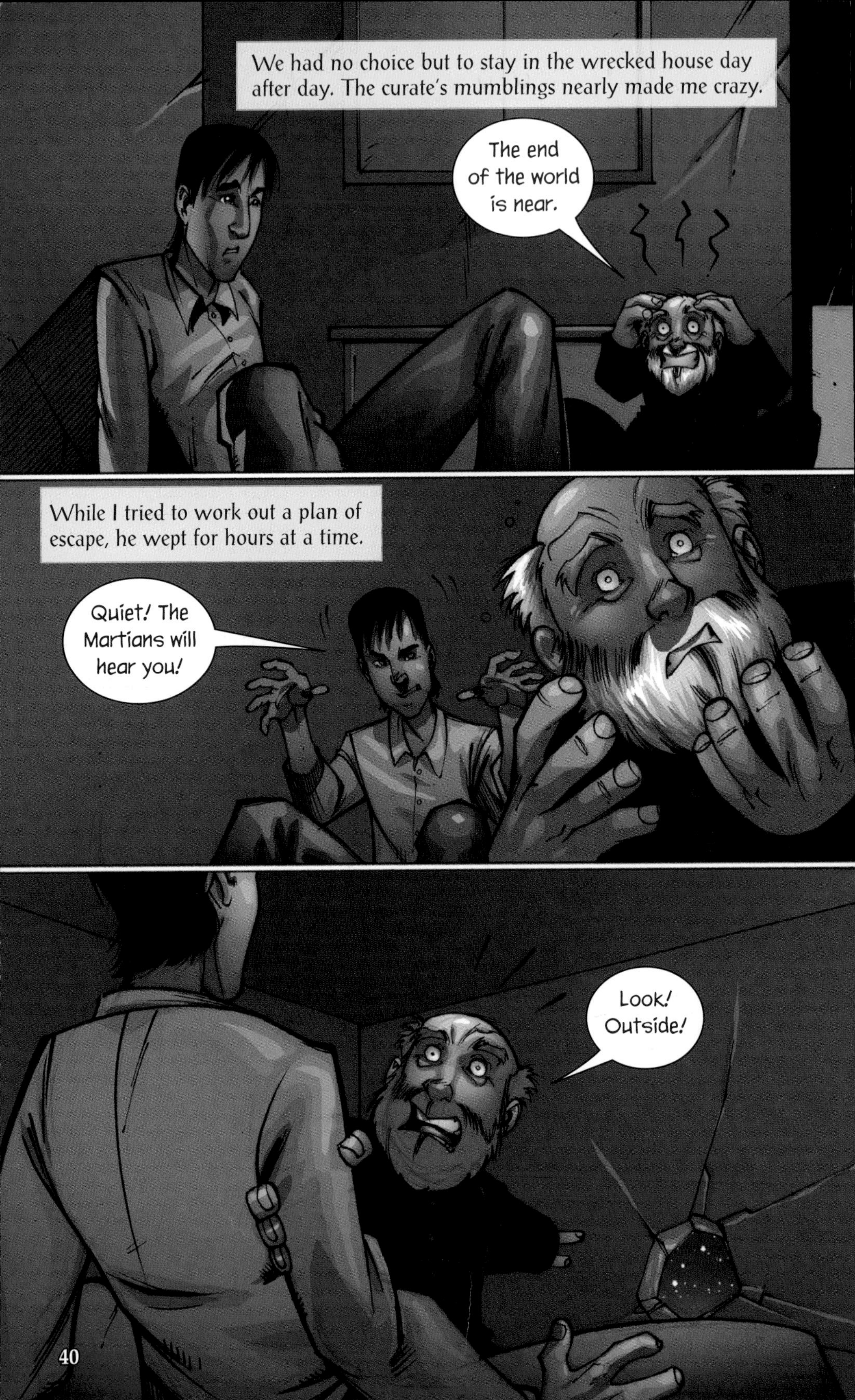
We had no choice but to stay in the wrecked house day after day. The curate's mumblings nearly made me crazy.
The end of the world is near.
While I tried to work out a plan of escape, he wept for hours at a time.
Quiet! The Martians will hear you!
Look! Outside!

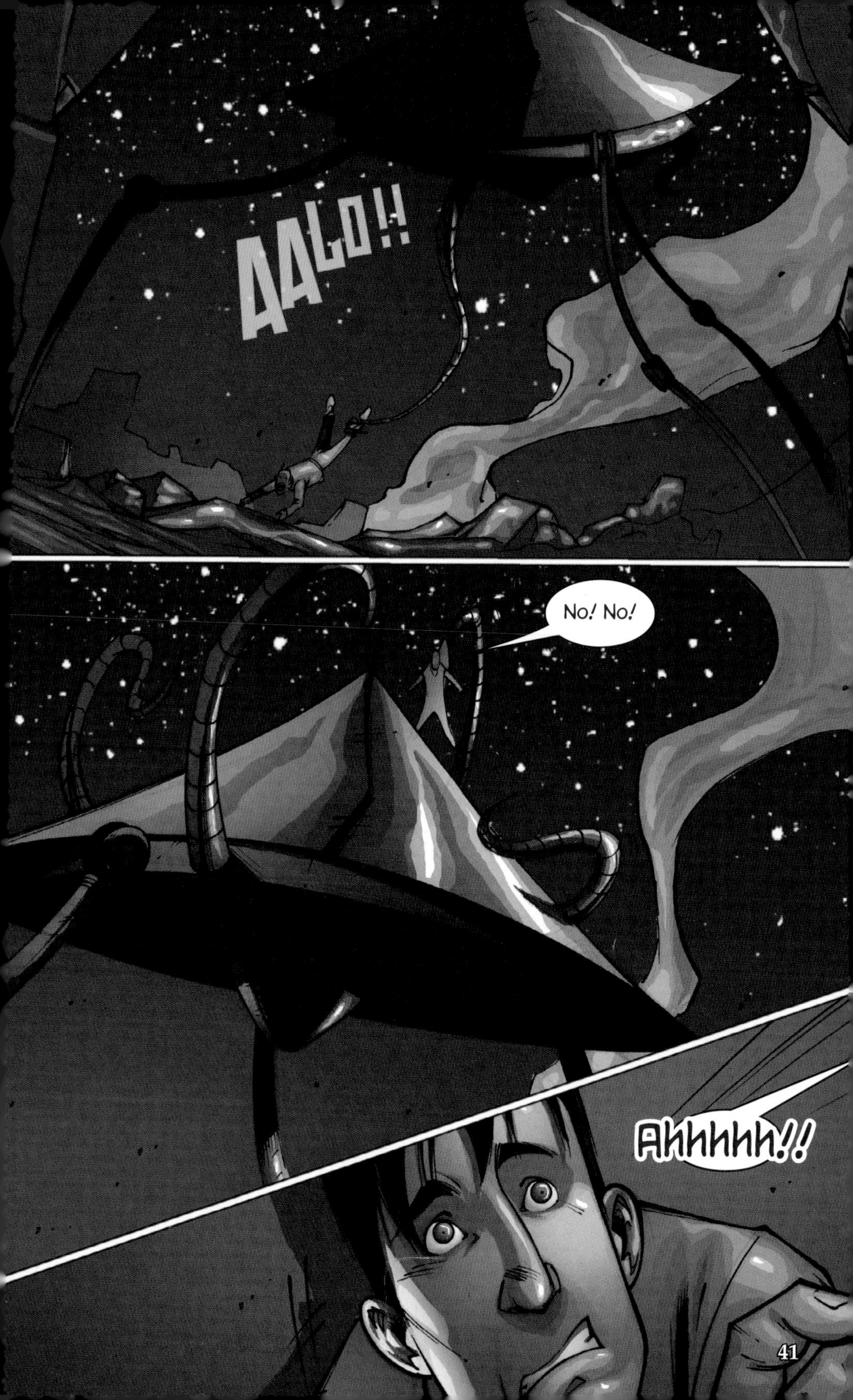
AALO!!
No! No!
Ahhhhh!!

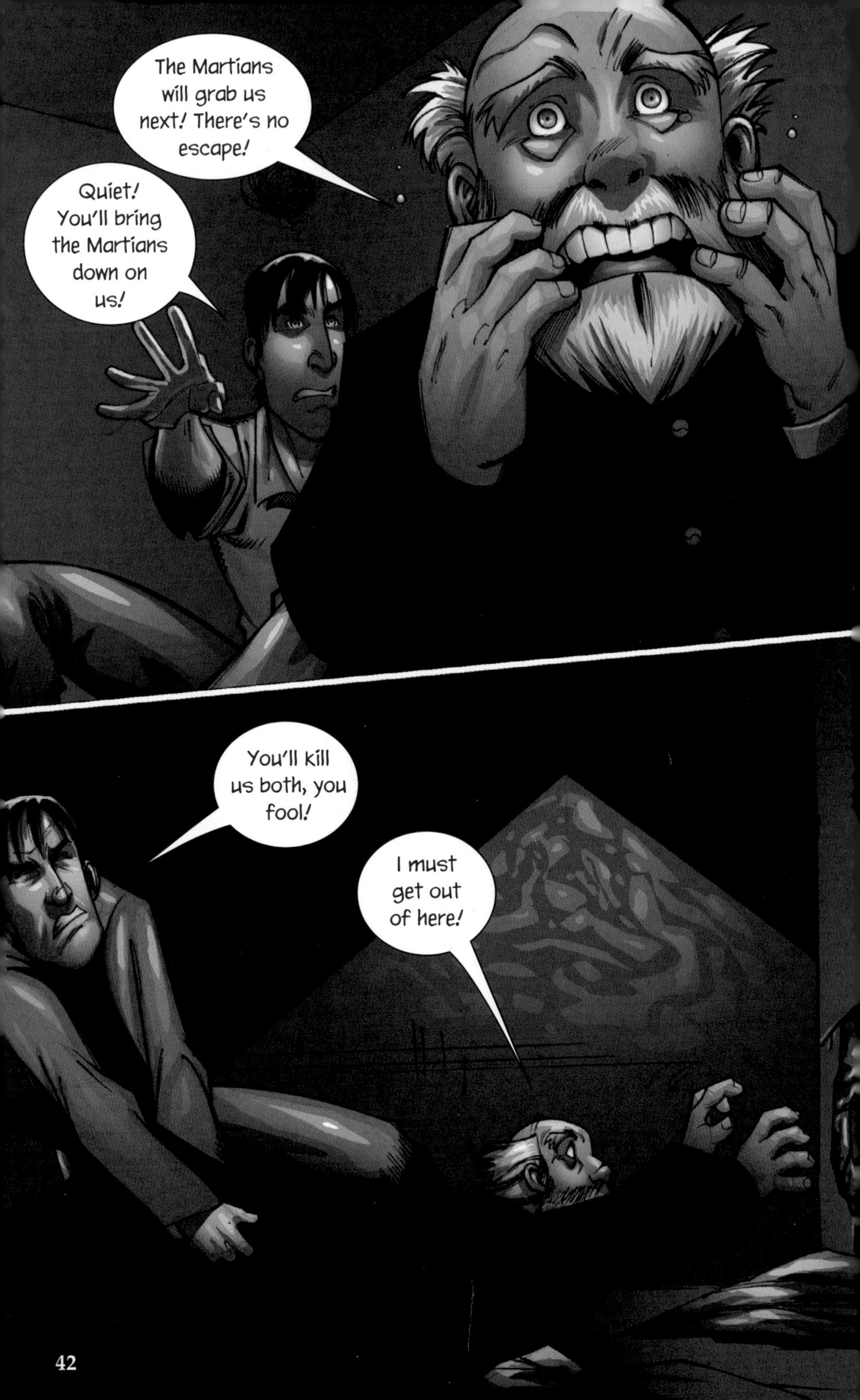
The Martians will grab us next! There's no escape!
Quiet! You'll bring the Martians down on us!
You'll kill us both, you fool!
I must get out of here!

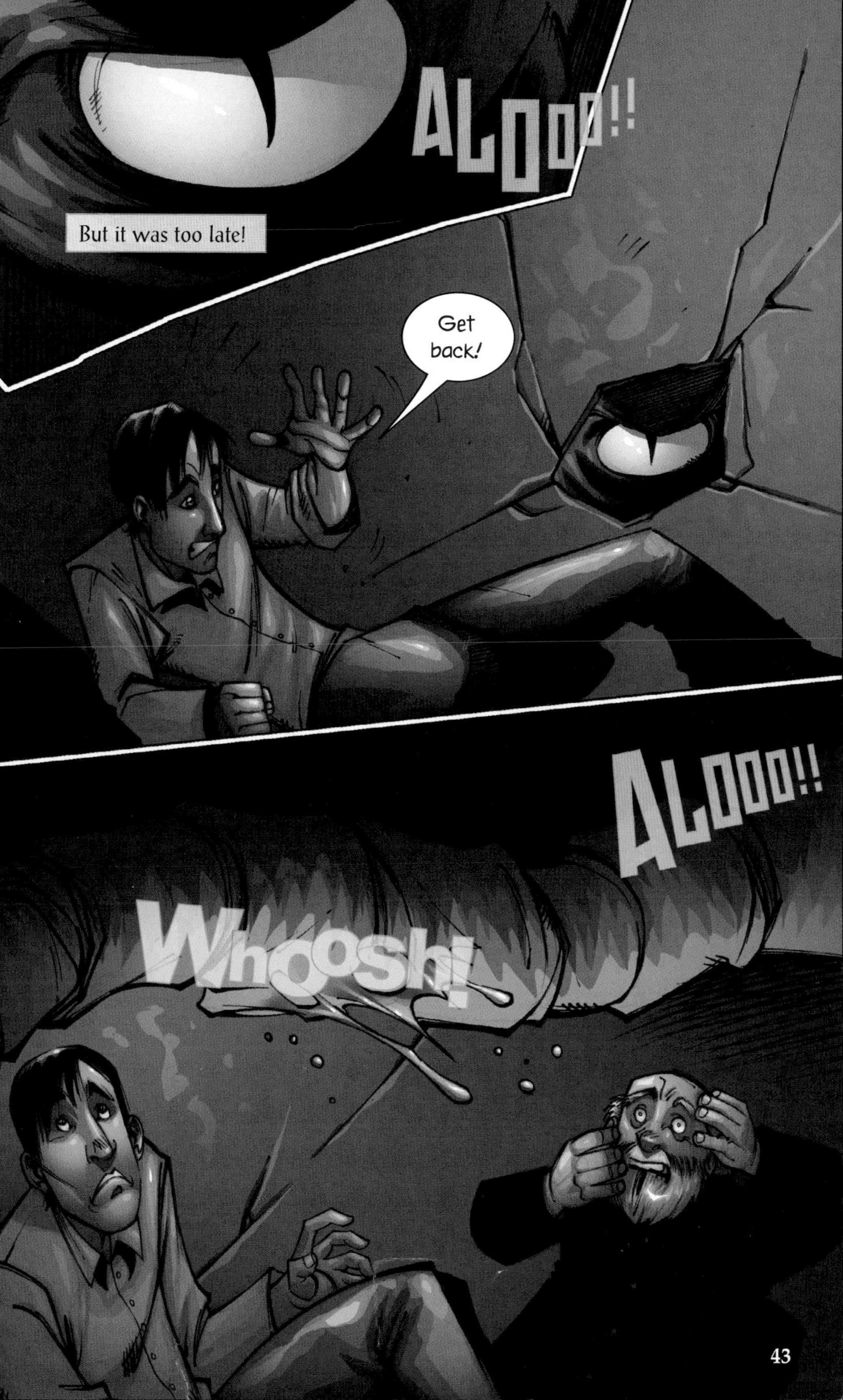
ALOOO!!
But it was too late!
Get back!
ALOOO!!
Whoosh!

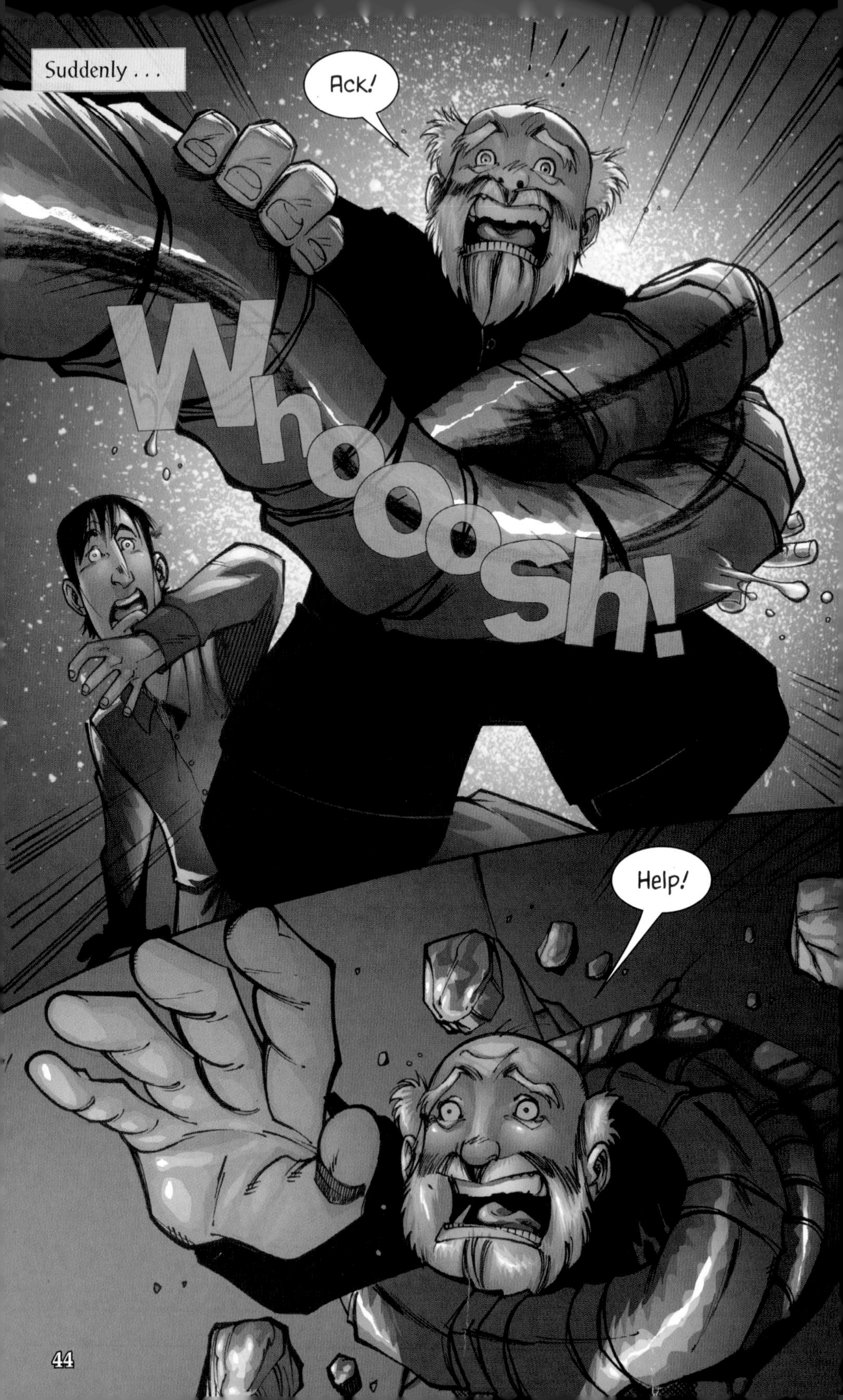

Suddenly . . .
Ack!
Whoooosh!
Help!

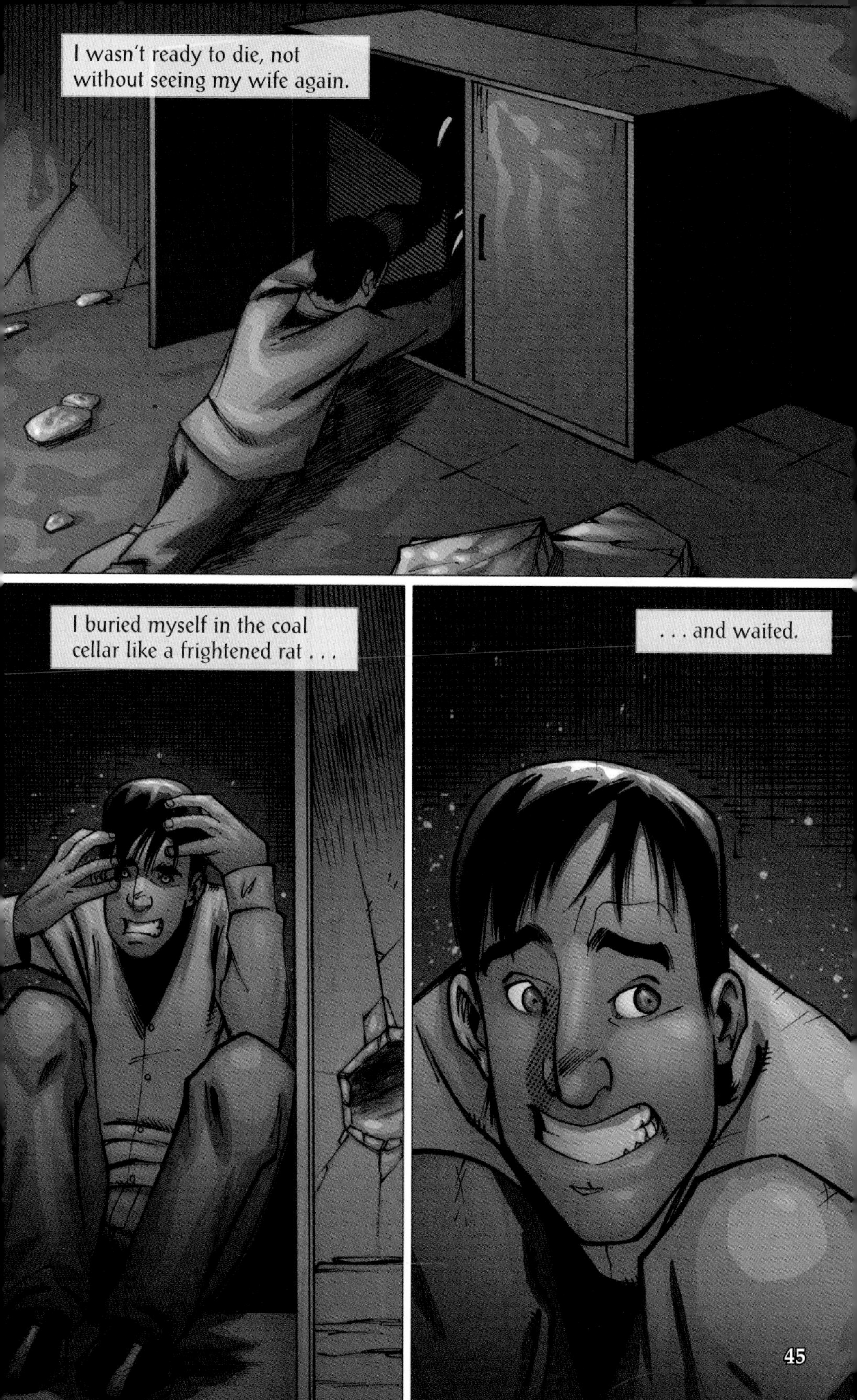
I wasn't ready to die, not without seeing my wife again.
I buried myself in the coal cellar like a frightened rat . . .
. . . and waited.

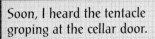

Soon, I heard the tentacle groping at the cellar door.

SLUuuRM

SLUuuRF

Then, it slithered inside, only inches from my face.

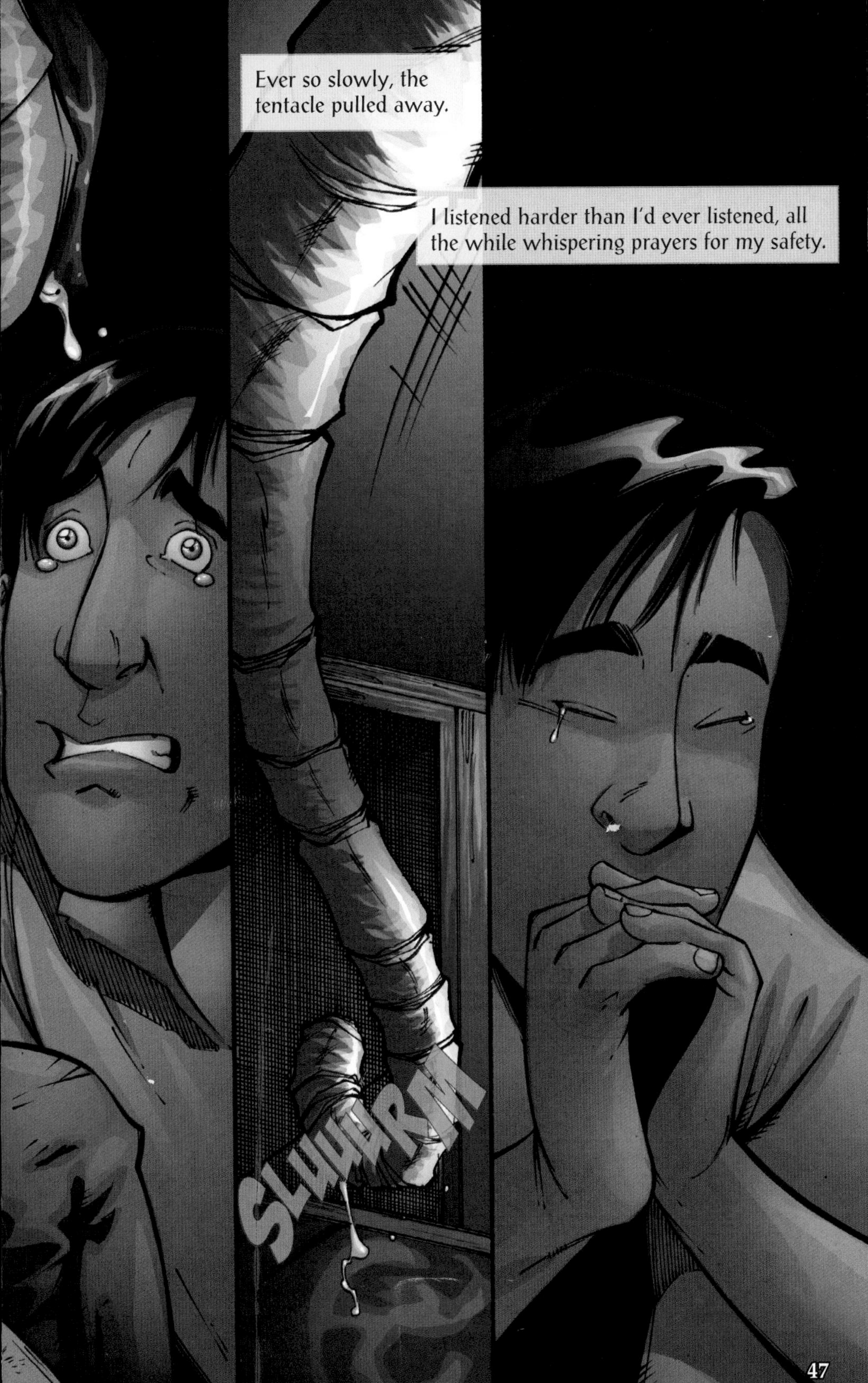
Ever so slowly, the tentacle pulled away.
SLUUURM
I listened harder than I'd ever listened, all the while whispering prayers for my safety.

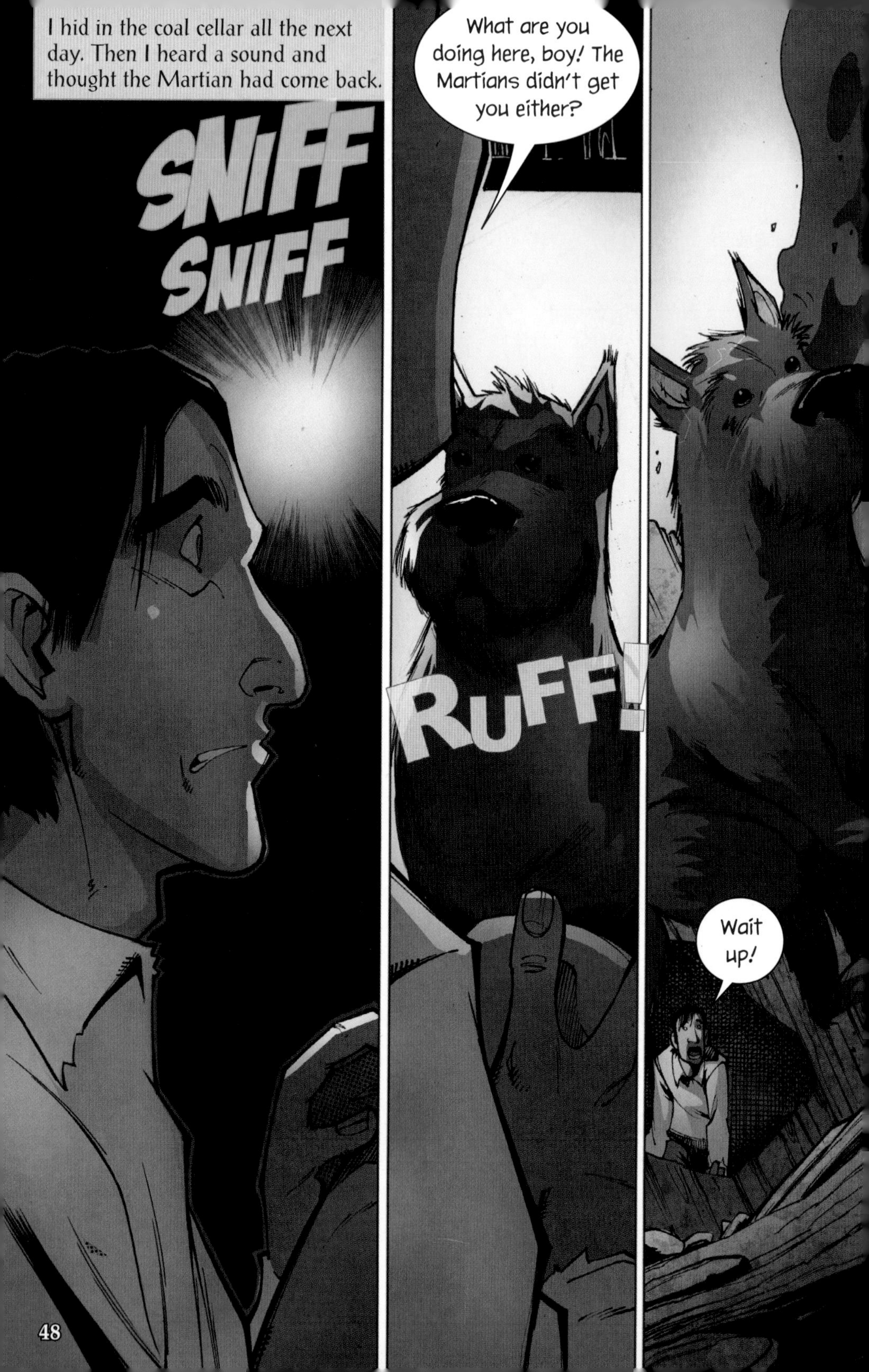

I hid in the coal cellar all the next day. Then I heard a sound and thought the Martian had come back.
SNIFF SNIFF
What are you doing here, boy! The Martians didn't get you either?
RUFF!
Wait up!

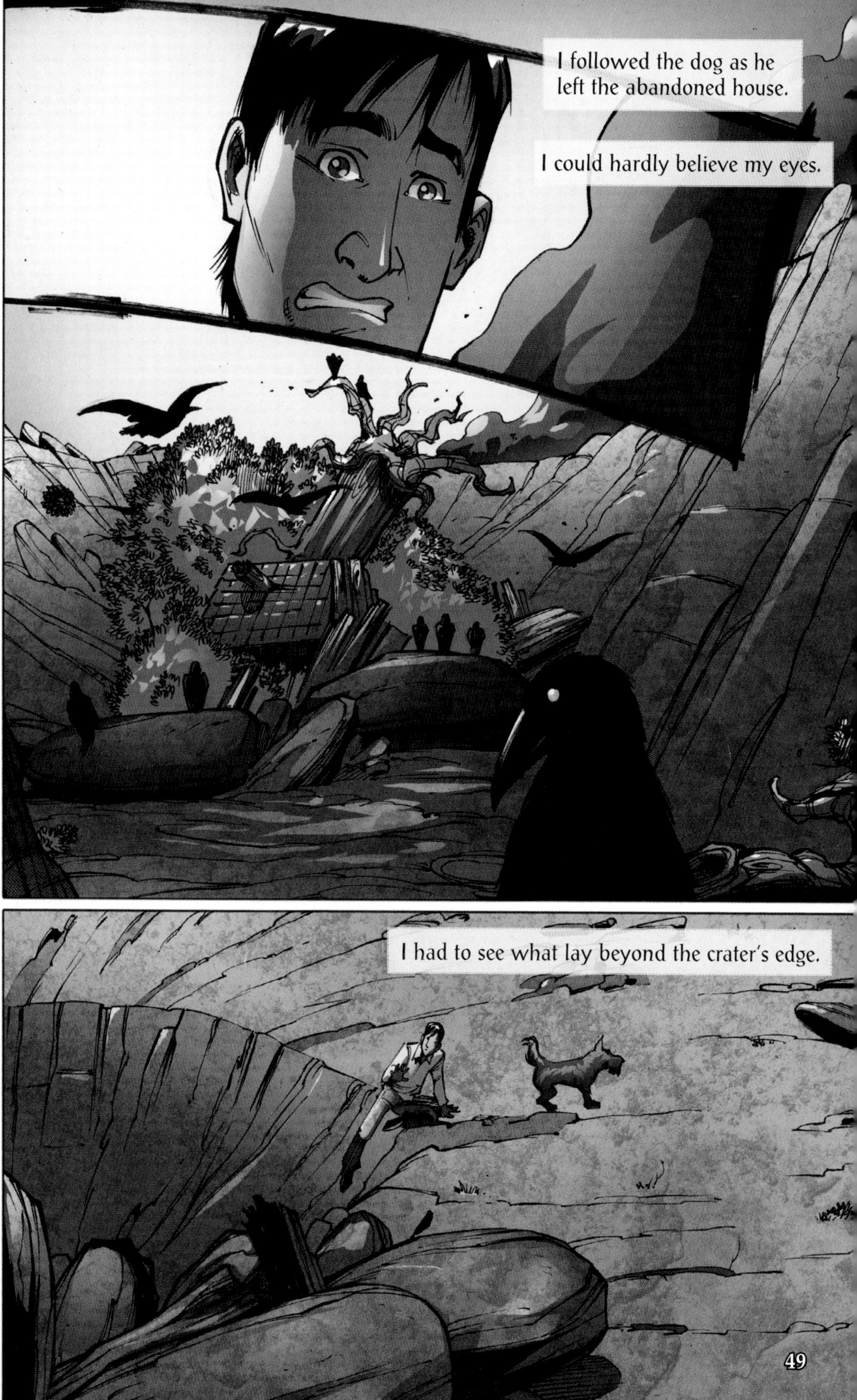
I followed the dog as he left the abandoned house.
I could hardly believe my eyes.
I had to see what lay beyond the crater's edge.

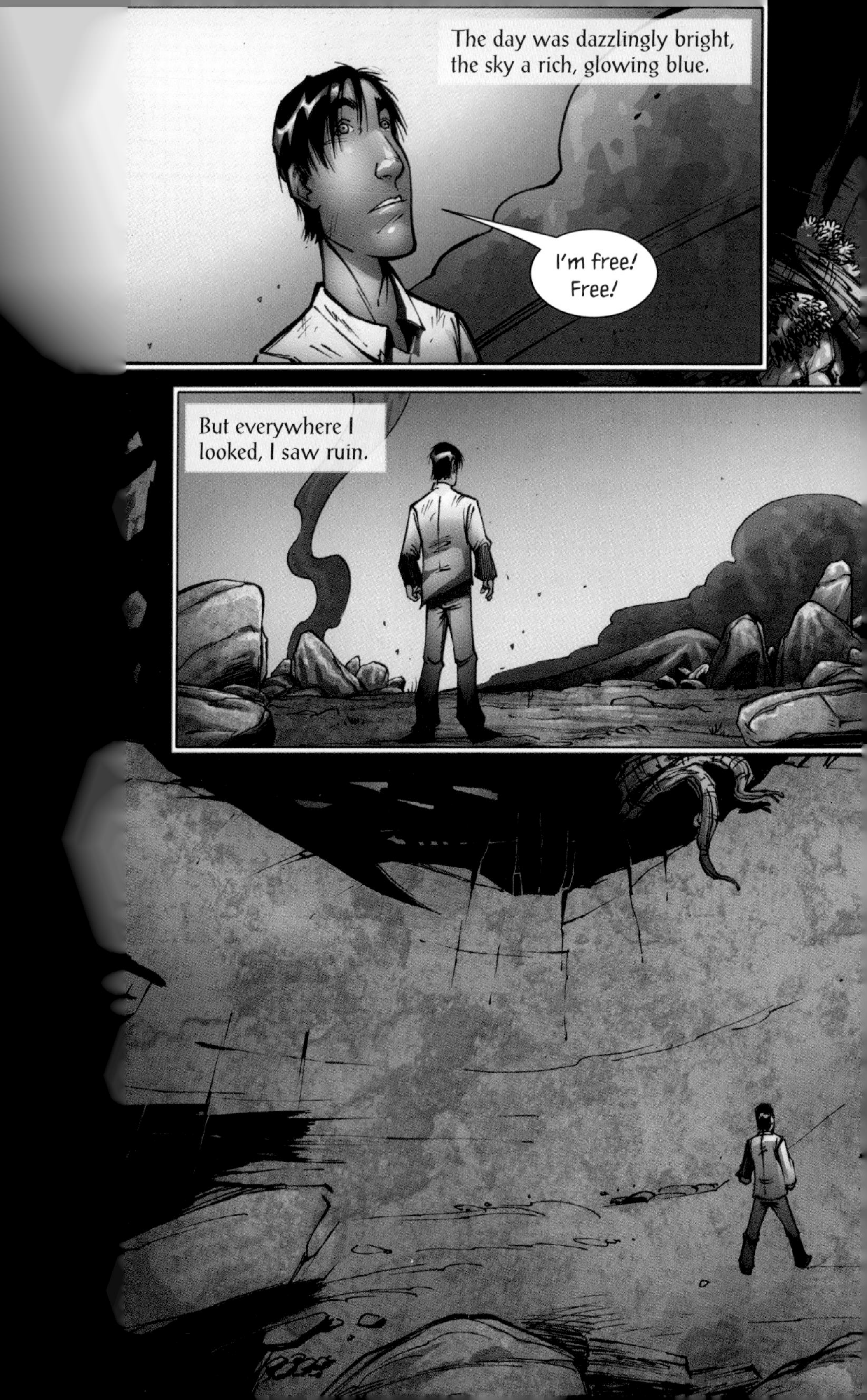
The day was dazzlingly bright, the sky a rich, glowing blue.
I'm free! Free!
But everywhere I looked, I saw ruin.

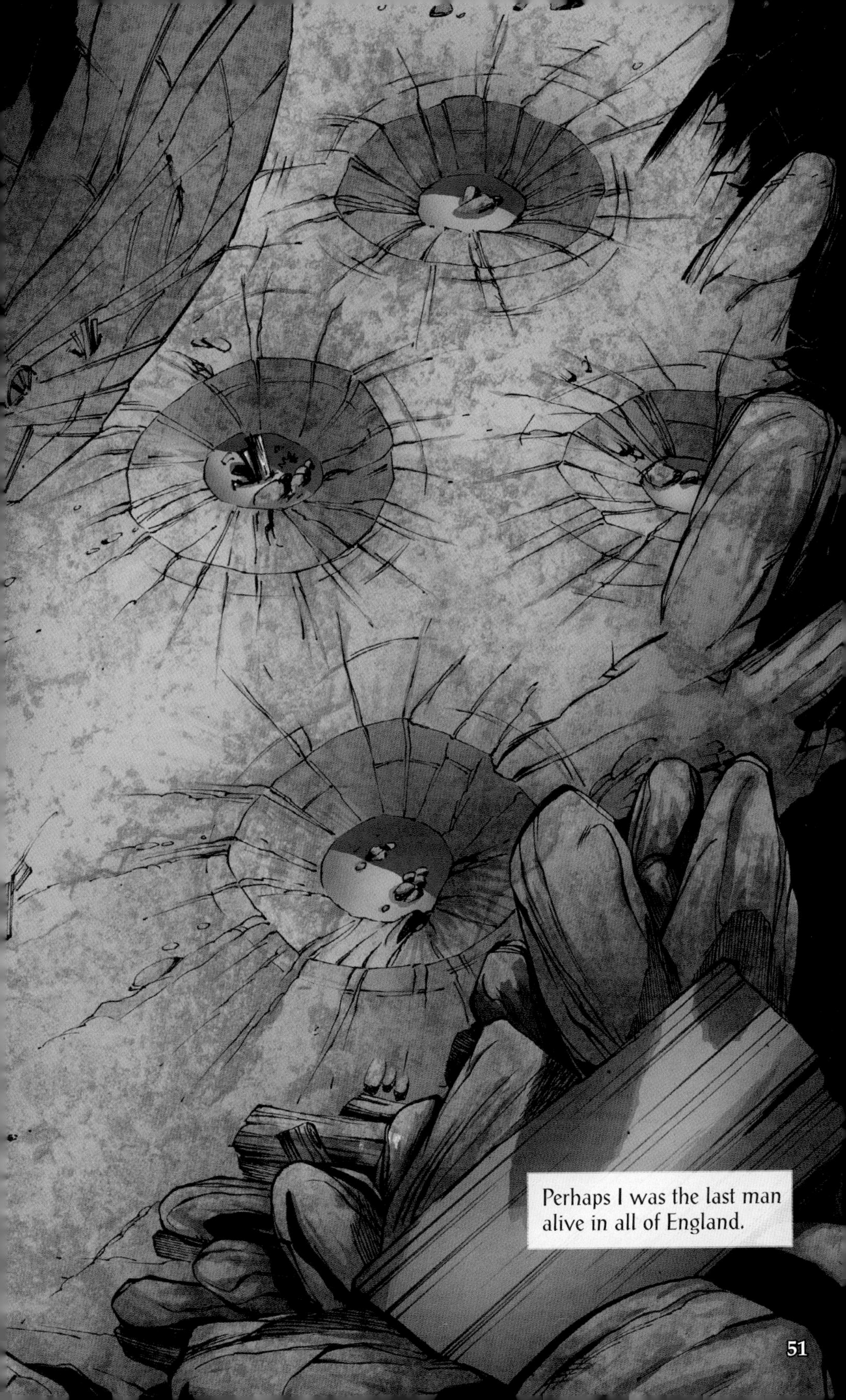
Perhaps I was the last man alive in all of England.

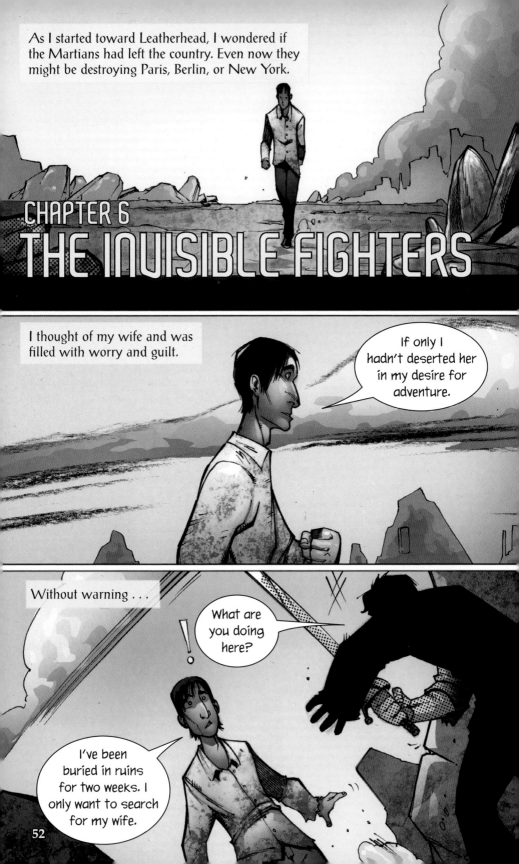

As I started toward Leatherhead, I wondered if the Martians had left the country. Even now they might be destroying Paris, Berlin, or New York.

CHAPTER 6
THE INVISIBLE FIGHTERS

I thought of my wife and was filled with worry and guilt.

If only I hadn't deserted her in my desire for adventure.

Without warning . . .

What are you doing here?

I've been buried in ruins for two weeks. I only want to search for my wife.

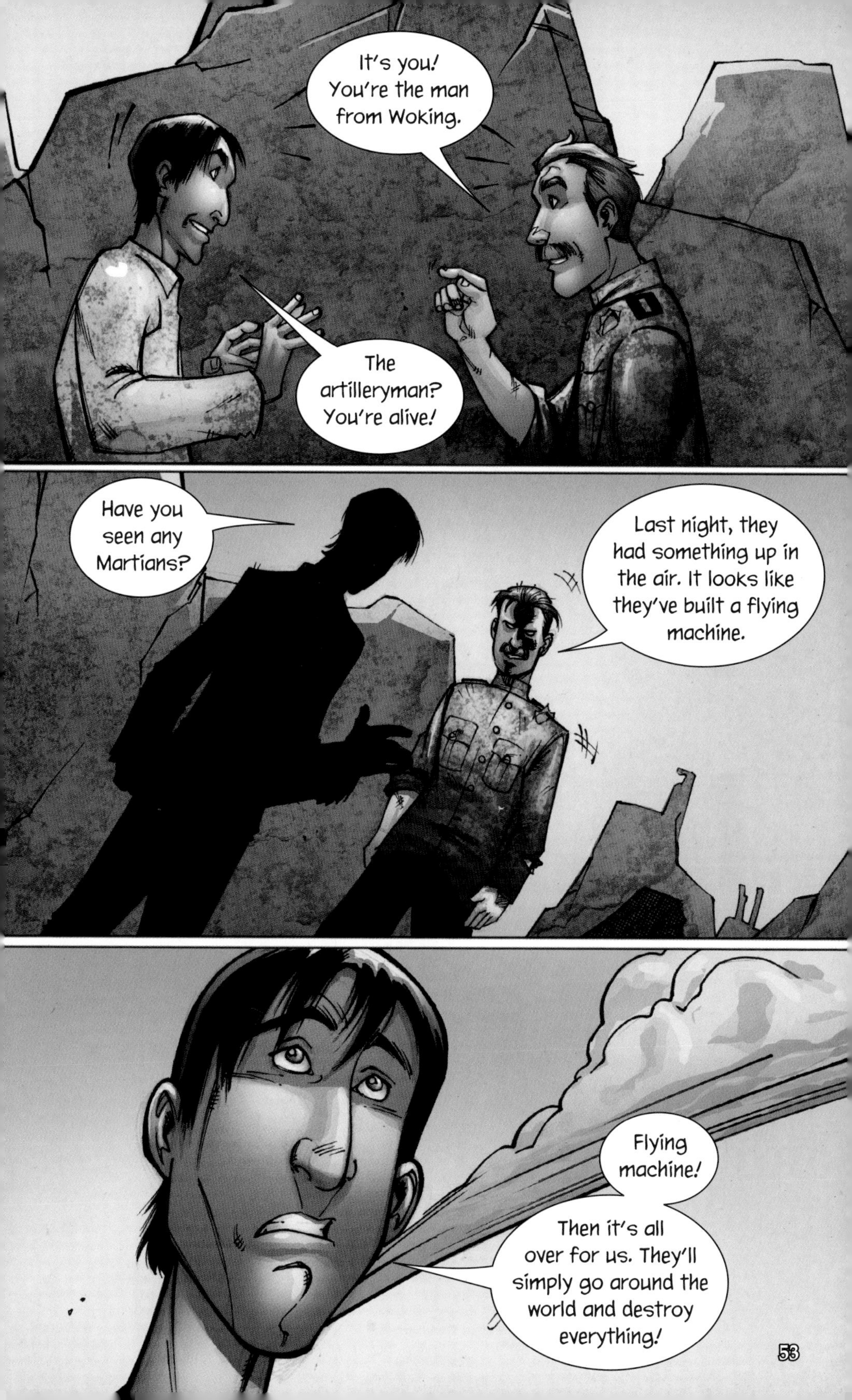
It's you! You're the man from Woking.
The artilleryman? You're alive!
Have you seen any Martians?
Last night, they had something up in the air. It looks like they've built a flying machine.
Flying machine!
Then it's all over for us. They'll simply go around the world and destroy everything!

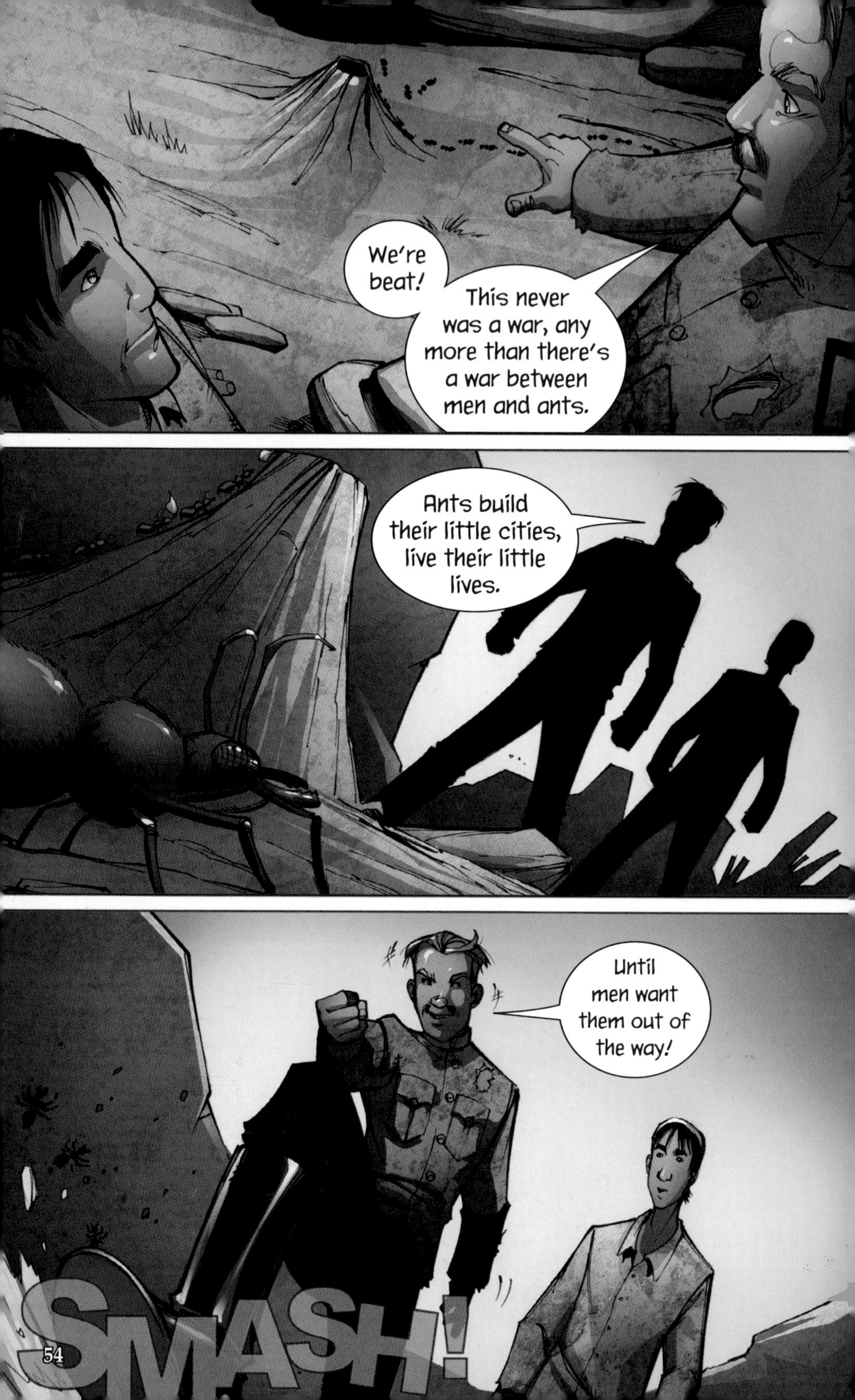
We're beat!
This never was a war, any more than there's a war between men and ants.
Ants build their little cities, live their little lives.
Until men want them out of the way!
SMASH!

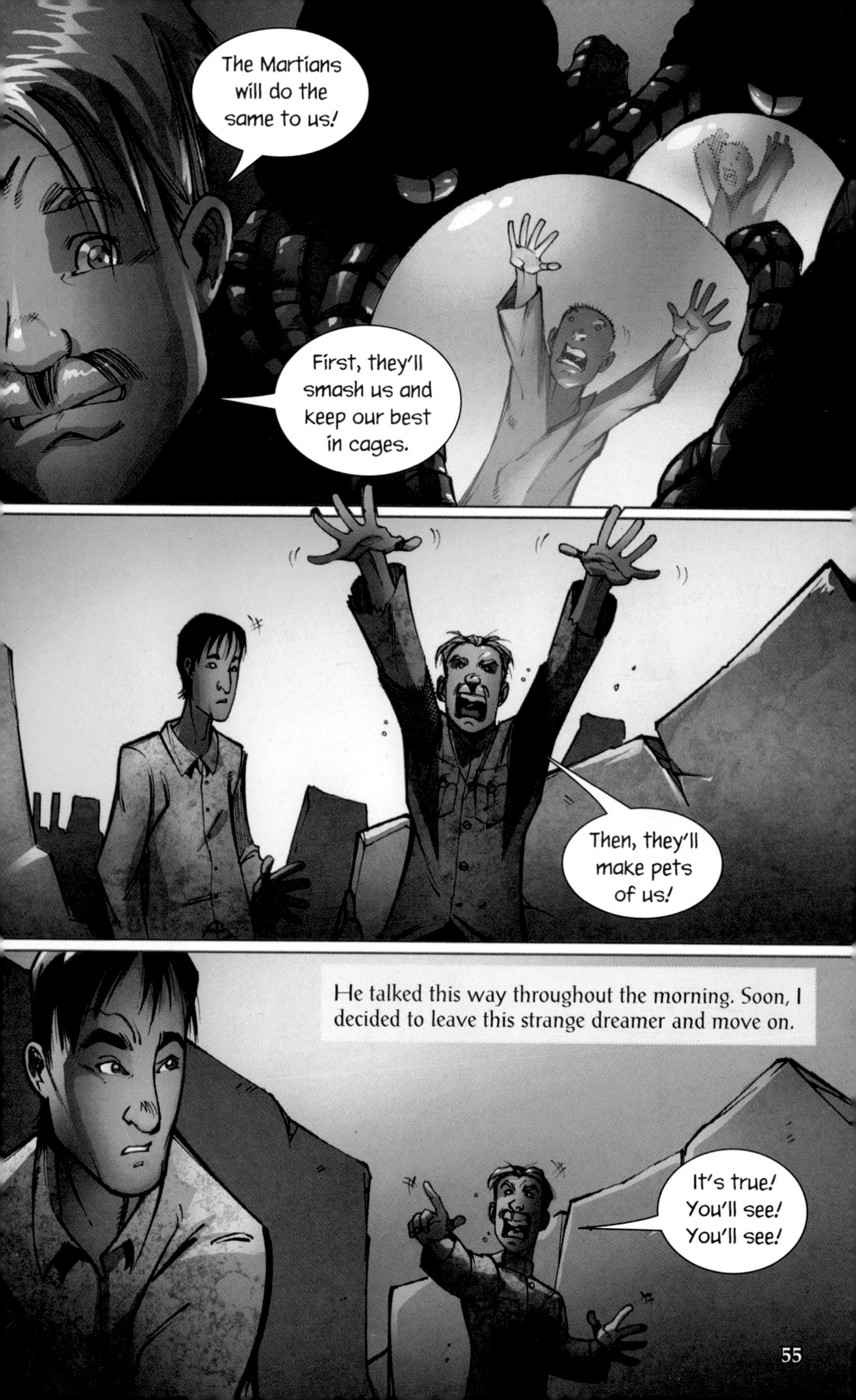
The Martians will do the same to us!
First, they'll smash us and keep our best in cages.
Then, they'll make pets of us!
He talked this way throughout the morning. Soon, I decided to leave this strange dreamer and move on.
It's true! You'll see! You'll see!

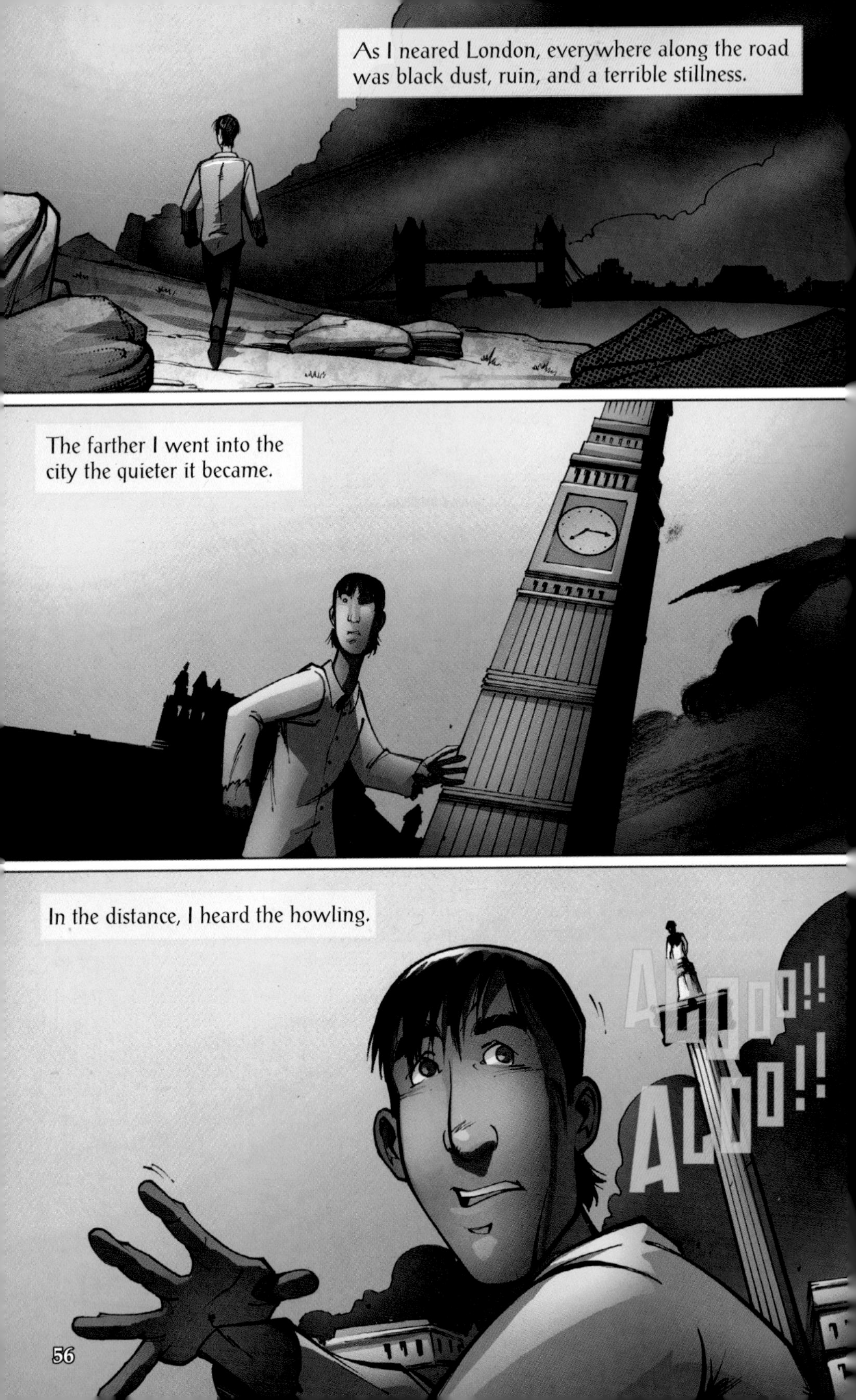

As I neared London, everywhere along the road was black dust, ruin, and a terrible stillness.
The farther I went into the city the quieter it became.
In the distance, I heard the howling.
ALOOO!!
ALOO!!

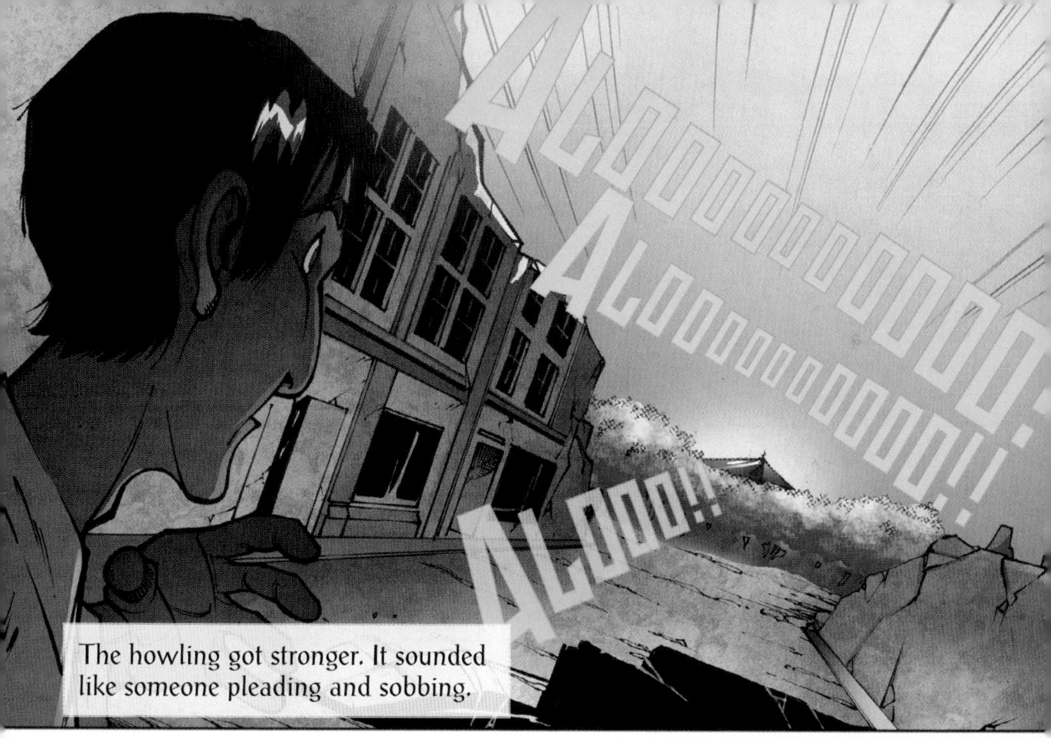
ALOOOOOOOOOOO!
ALOOOOOOOOOOO!!
ALOOO!!
The howling got stronger. It sounded like someone pleading and sobbing.

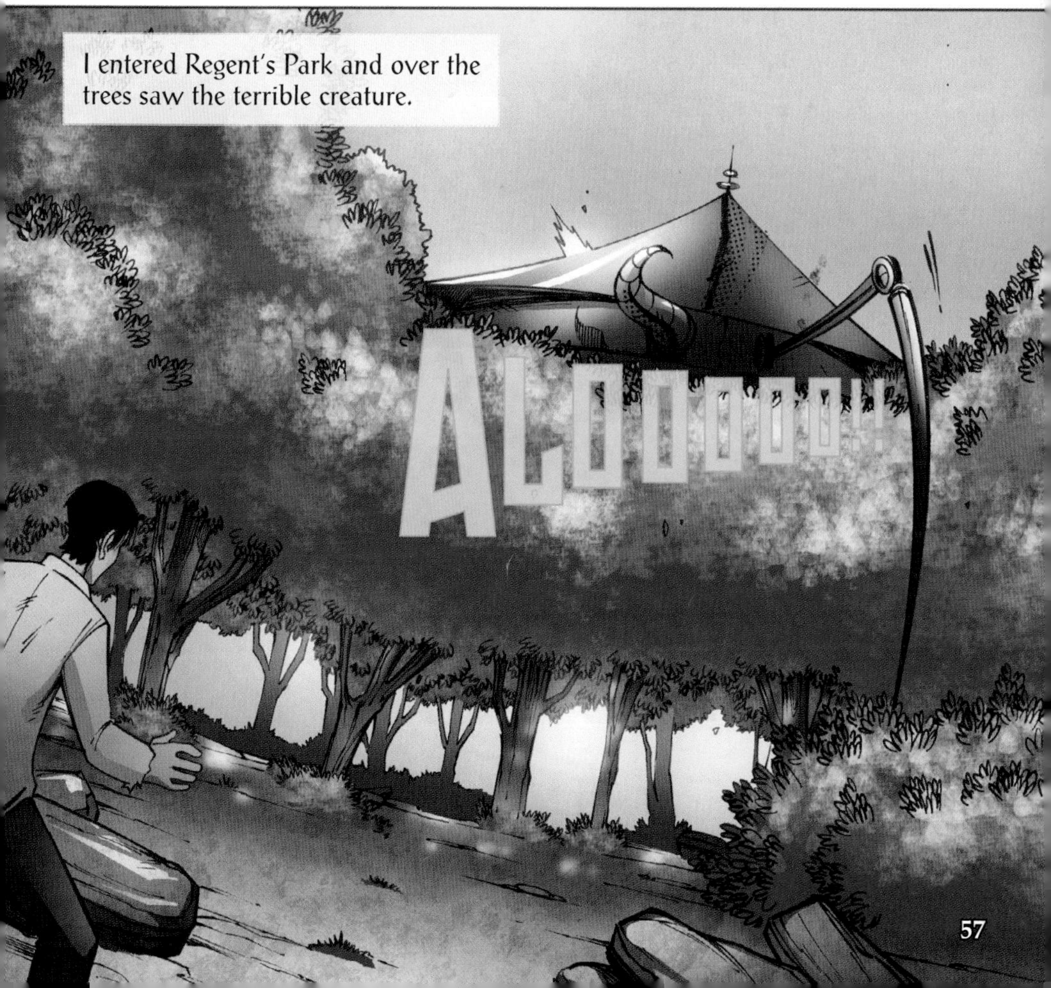
I entered Regent's Park and over the trees saw the terrible creature.
ALOOOOOO!!

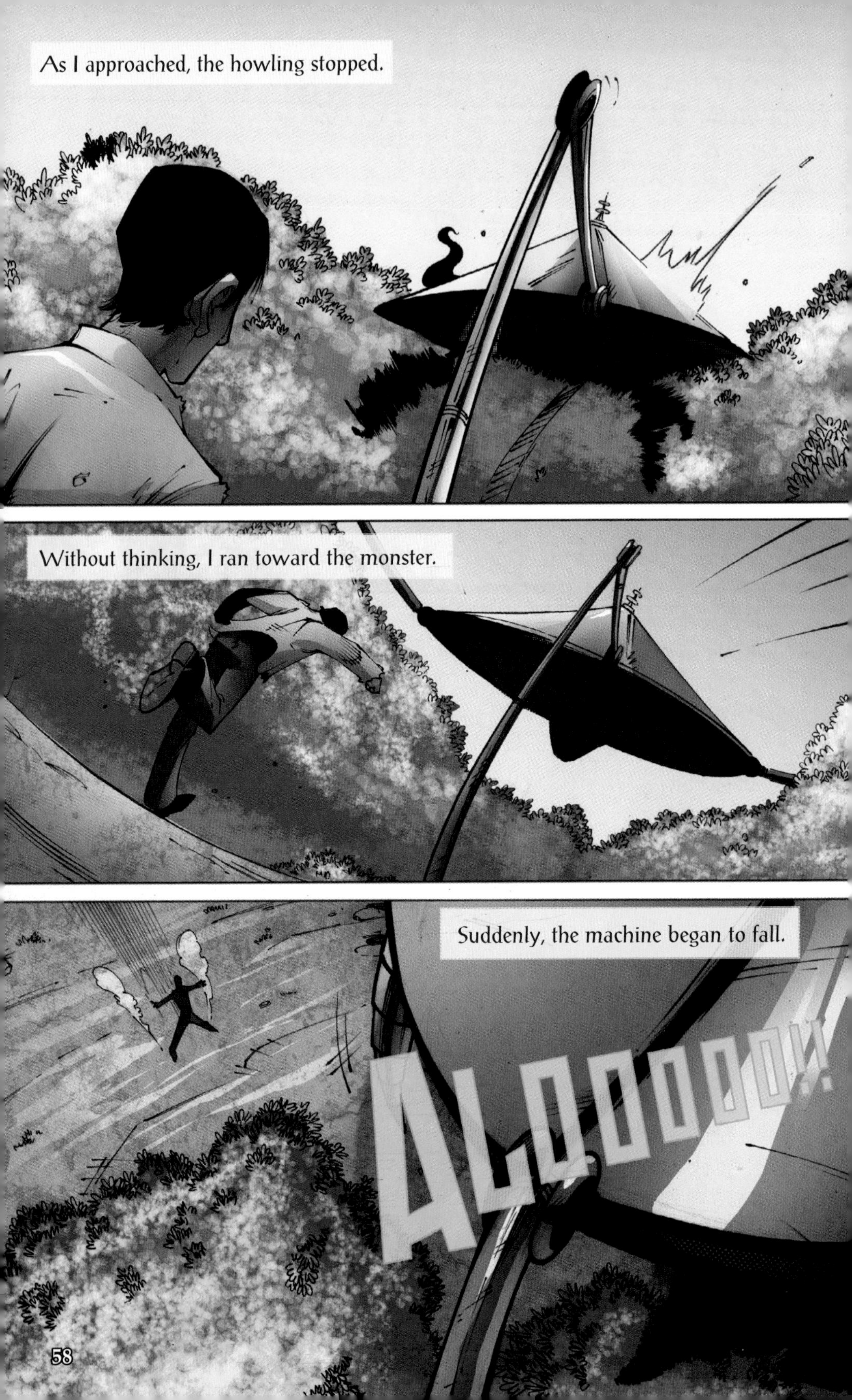
As I approached, the howling stopped.
Without thinking, I ran toward the monster.
Suddenly, the machine began to fall.
ALOOOOO!!

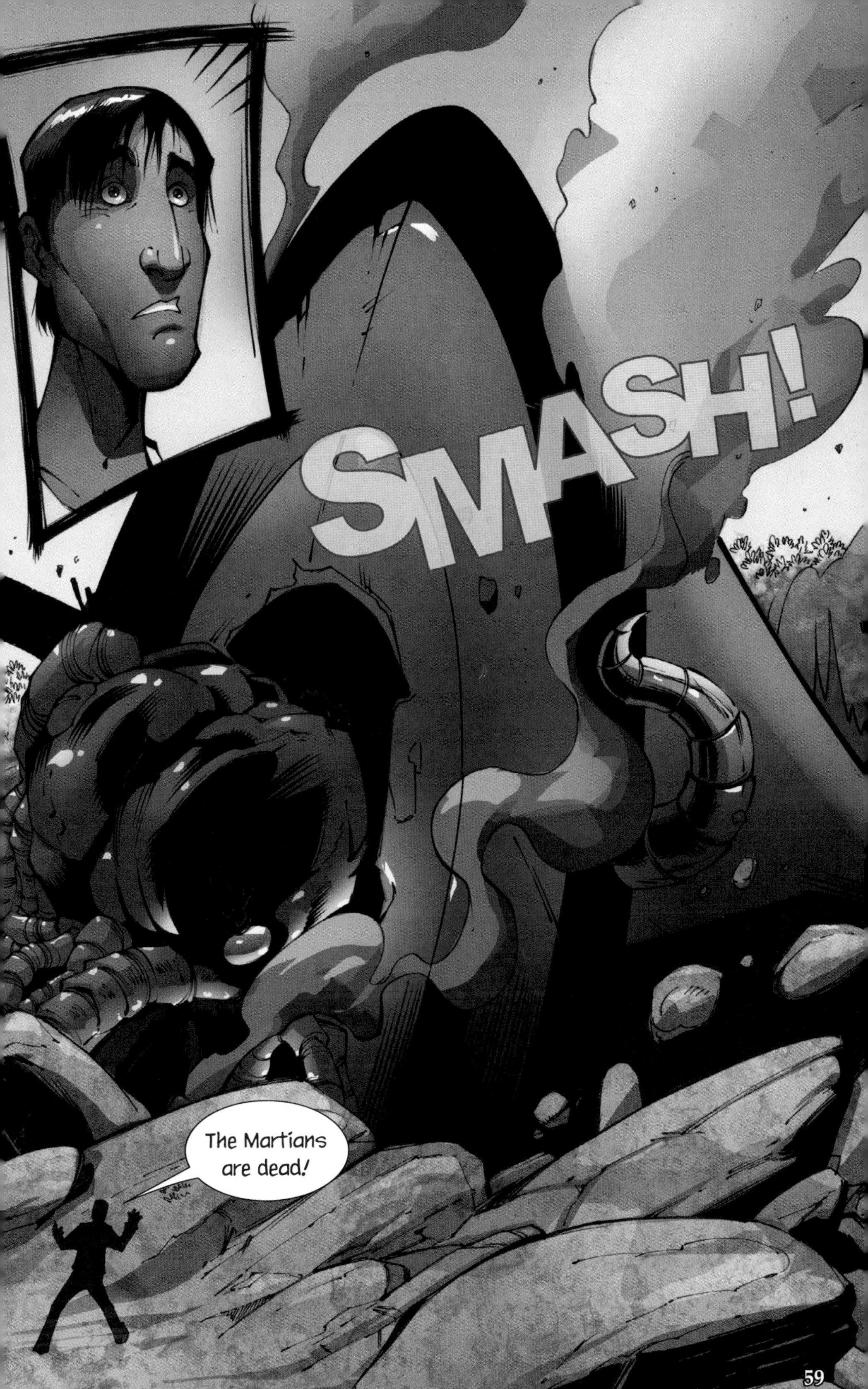
SMASH!
The Martians are dead!

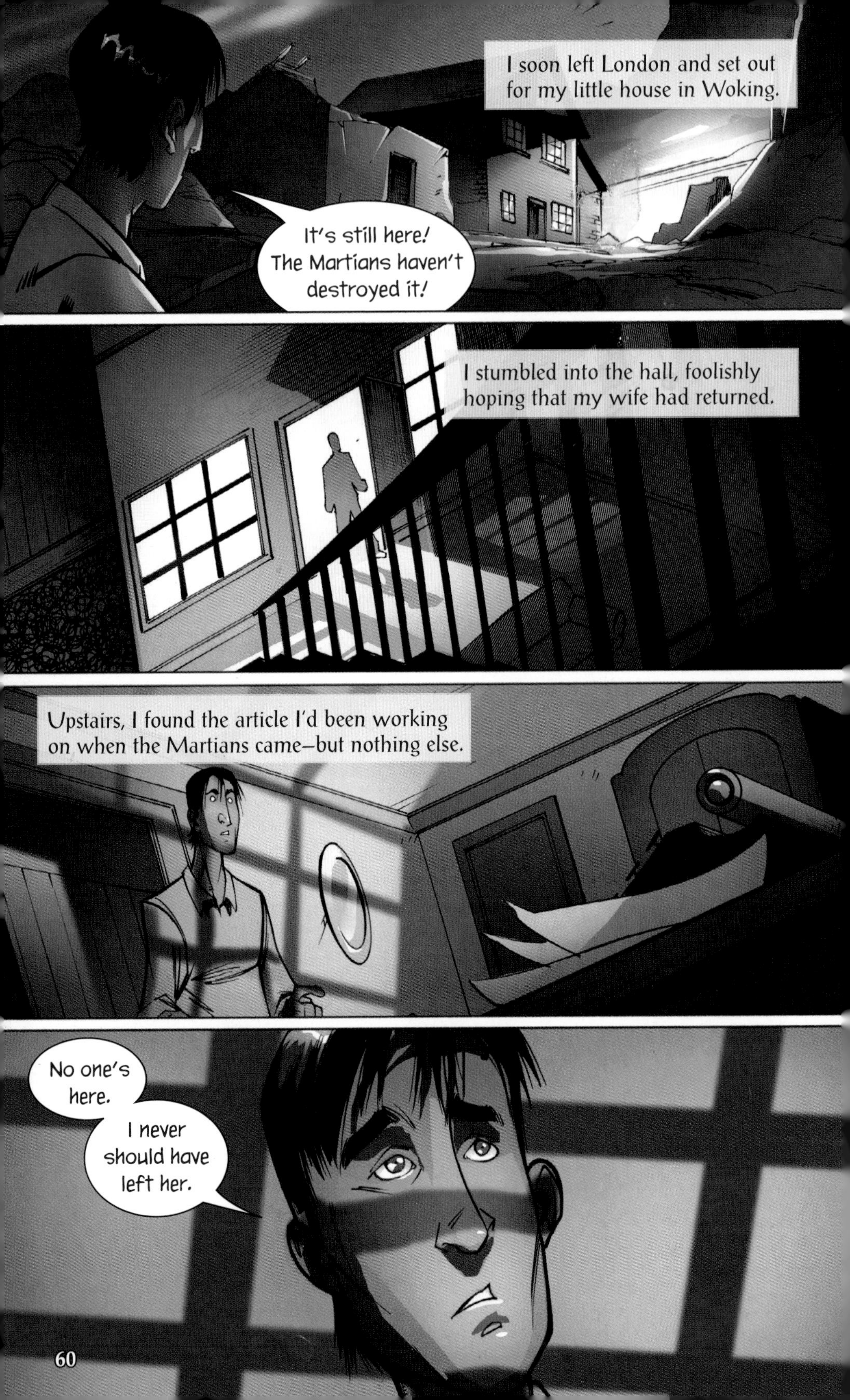
I soon left London and set out for my little house in Woking.
It's still here! The Martians haven't destroyed it!
I stumbled into the hall, foolishly hoping that my wife had returned.
Upstairs, I found the article I'd been working on when the Martians came—but nothing else.
No one's here.
I never should have left her.

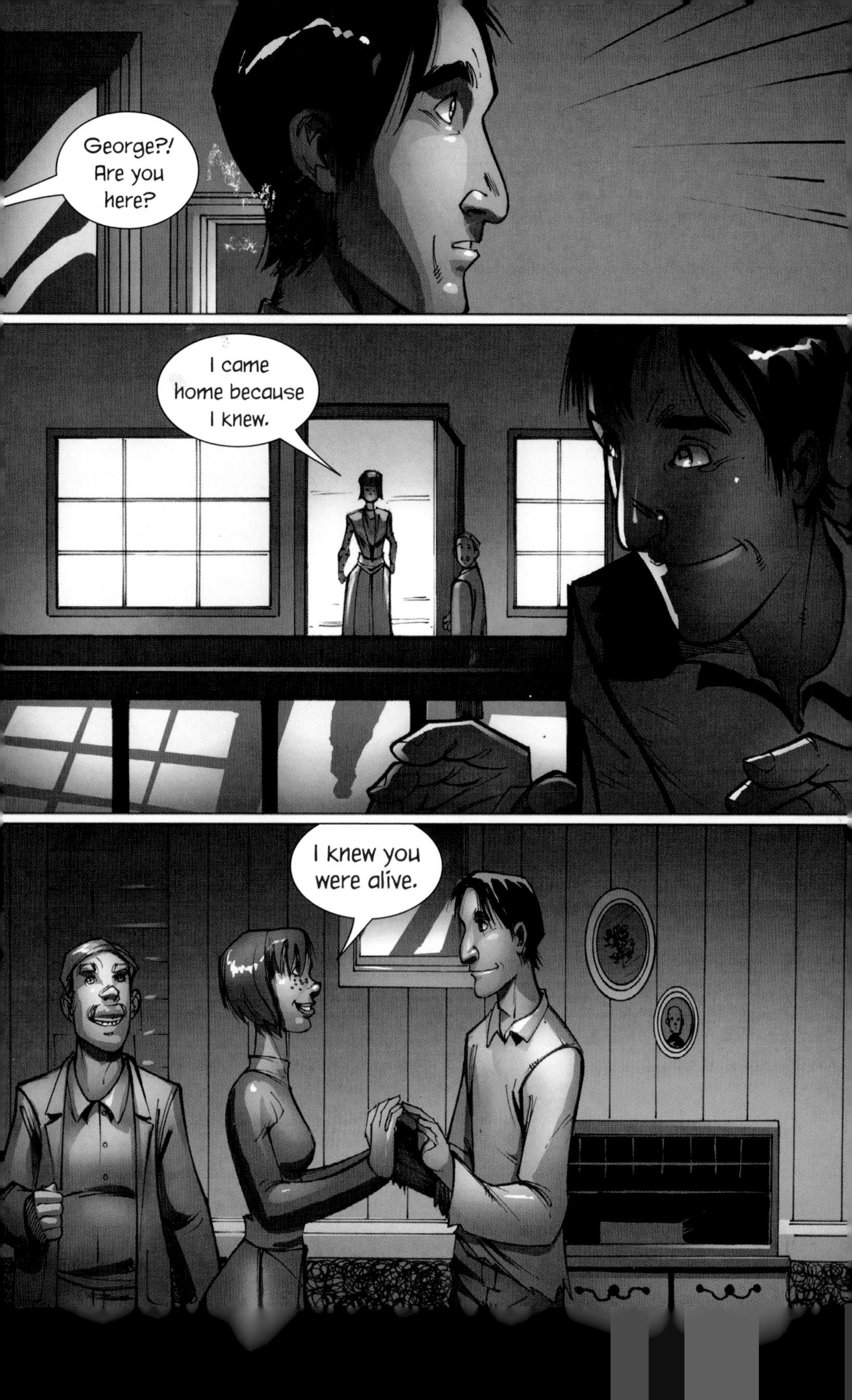
George?! Are you here?
I came home because I knew.
I knew you were alive.

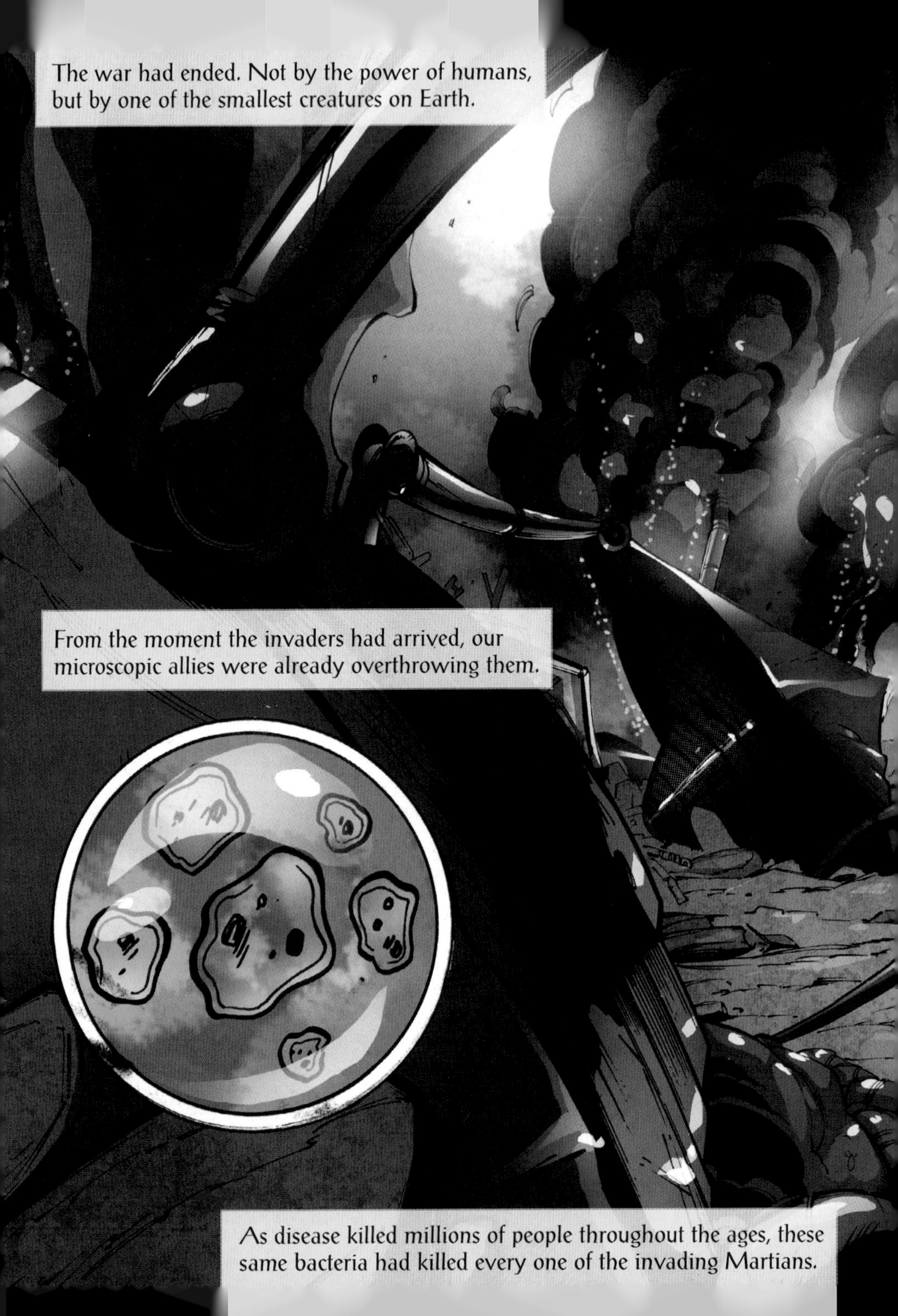

The war had ended. Not by the power of humans, but by one of the smallest creatures on Earth.
From the moment the invaders had arrived, our microscopic allies were already overthrowing them.
As disease killed millions of people throughout the ages, these same bacteria had killed every one of the invading Martians.

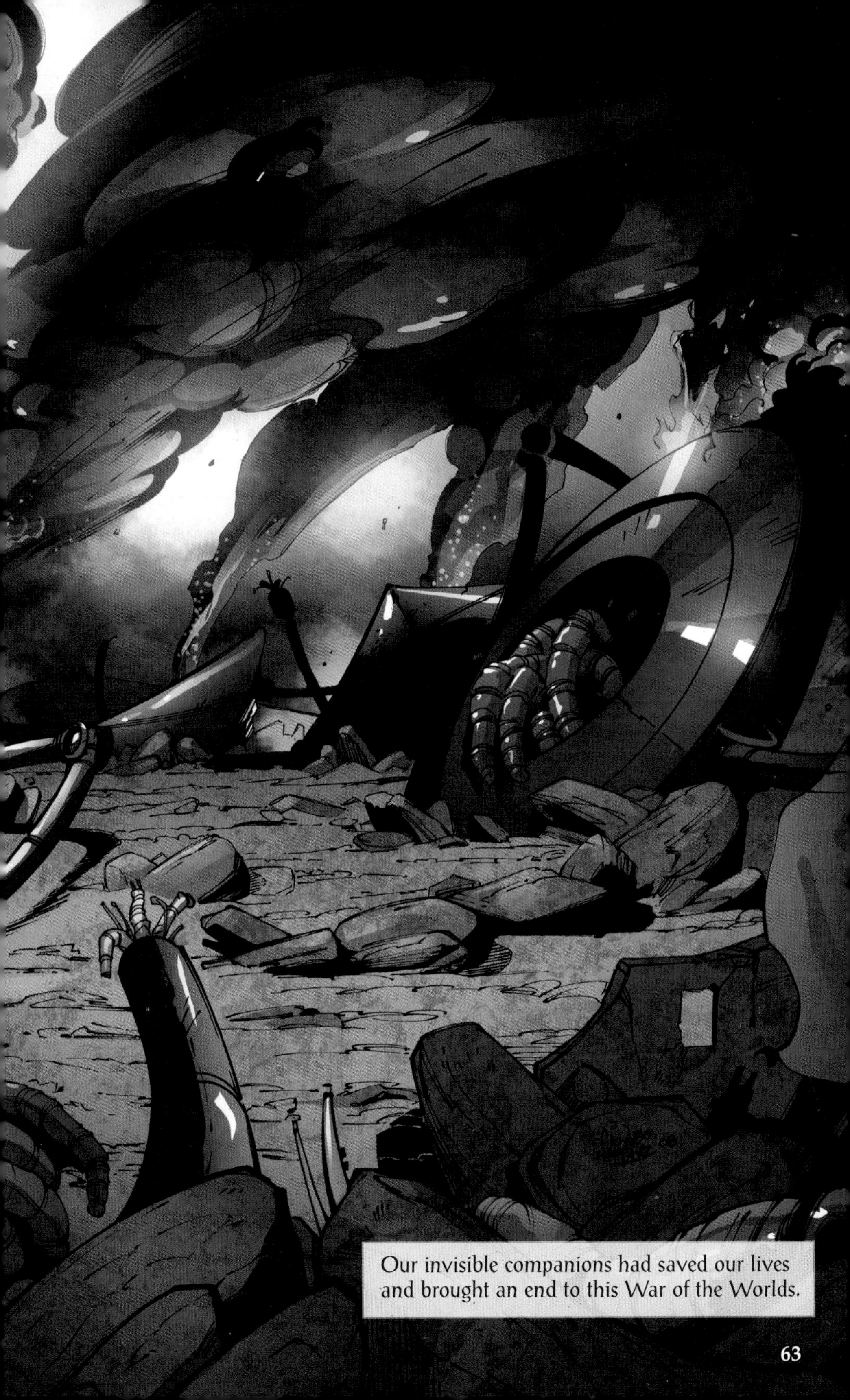
Our invisible companions had saved our lives and brought an end to this War of the Worlds.

About the Author

Herbert George Wells was born on September 21, 1866, in England. At age 7, he suffered a broken leg. While resting his injury, Wells started reading books. As he grew older, he continued to enjoy reading and school. At 14, young Wells quit school to help his struggling family. Fortunately, he received a scholarship in 1883 and began studying science at a school in London. Soon after, Wells started writing. Some of his works, like *The War of the Worlds*, combine his love for storytelling and science.

About the Retelling Authors

Davis Worth Miller and Katherine McLean Brevar are a married couple living and working together in North Carolina. They are both full-time writers. Miller has written several best-selling books including *The Tao of Muhammad Ali.* He is now working on his memoir and several other novels with his wife.

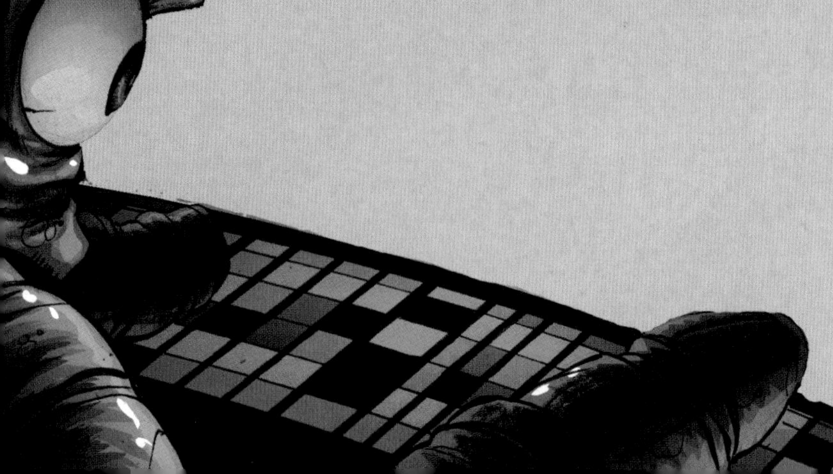

Glossary

abandoned (uh-BAN-duhnd)—empty, or no longer in use

allies (AL-eyes)—people or things that give support and help to another

bacteria (bak-TIHR-ee-uh)—microscopic living things that sometimes cause disease

crater (KRAY-tur)—a large hole in the ground often caused by an explosion

curate (KYOO-rayt)—a person in charge of a church

cylinder (SIL-uhn-dur)—a shape with flat, circular ends and sides shaped like the outside of a tube

gravity (GRAV-uh-tee)—the force that pulls things down toward Earth and keeps them from floating into space

Martians (MAR-shuhns)—fictional alien creatures from the planet Mars

meteorite (MEE-tee-ur-rite)—the part of a meteor or space rock that falls to Earth before it has burned up

microscopic (mye-kruh-SKOP-ik)—too small to be seen without a microscope

tentacle (TEN-tuh-kuhl)—one of the long, flexible limbs of some animals, such as an octopus

An Invasion from Mars!

On October 30, 1938, an announcer for CBS Radio started his broadcast with a warning. He told his listeners that for the next 60 minutes they'd be hearing a play based on the H.G. Wells novel, *The War of the Worlds*. Unfortunately, many people tuned in late and never heard the introduction.

As the show started, the radio's music was quickly interrupted by a breaking news bulletin. It said a "huge flaming object" had struck a farm near Grover's Mill, New Jersey. A reporter on the scene described seeing an alien crawl out of a spacecraft. "Good heavens, something's wriggling out of the shadow," he said. "I can see the thing's body now. It's large—large as a bear. It glistens like wet leather."

Later reports detailed that Newark, New Jersey, had been destroyed by Martian invaders. The reports stated that the aliens were on their way to New York City, which was being evacuated. Other flaming objects and invaders had been spotted near Washington, Buffalo, Chicago, and other cities around the country.

Of course, all of these "reports" of aliens were just part of the radio show. Still, thousands of people believed the attacks were real. They called newspapers, radio stations, and police headquarters, asking how to protect themselves from the aliens.

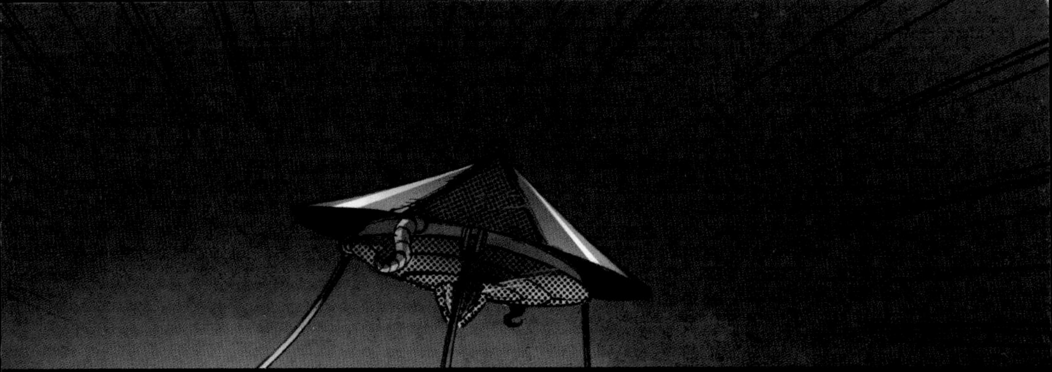

Hundreds of people needed medical treatment for shock. Terrified listeners hid in their cellars and loaded their rifles. In the area around New York City, highways became jammed with cars. Train and bus stations were choked with terrified people trying to leave the city.

In all, about one million people believed that they were listening to a real alien invasion. As the show ended, those people soon realized that they had been tricked. The entire show was simply a Halloween gag performed by 23-year-old Orson Welles and a group of actors. Welles would later become one of the most famous movie directors in Hollywood.

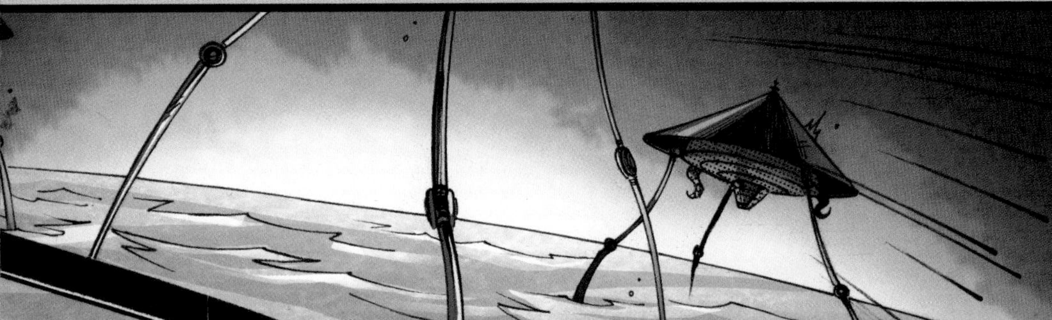

Discussion Questions

1. On page 21, George leaves his wife to go hunt for the Martians. Do you think this was a good decision? Or, do you think he should have stayed with her? Explain your answer.

2. At the end of the story, the Martians that came to Earth are defeated. Do you think more of them will come? Why or why not?

3. This story is fiction, but do you think aliens really exist? Do you think they will ever come to Earth? Will they be good or evil? Explain your answers.

Writing Prompts

1. An alien spacecraft has just landed in your town! Would you be friendly to the aliens or try to make them go away? Write a story about what you would do.

2. Describe what you think an alien creature would look like. When you're finished writing out the description, give it to a friend. Have him or her draw a picture of the creature based on your description. Did the alien turn out like you imagined?

3. The aliens in this book came from Mars. Describe what you think the cities on their planet look like. Where do the aliens live? Where do they eat? Do the alien kids go to school?

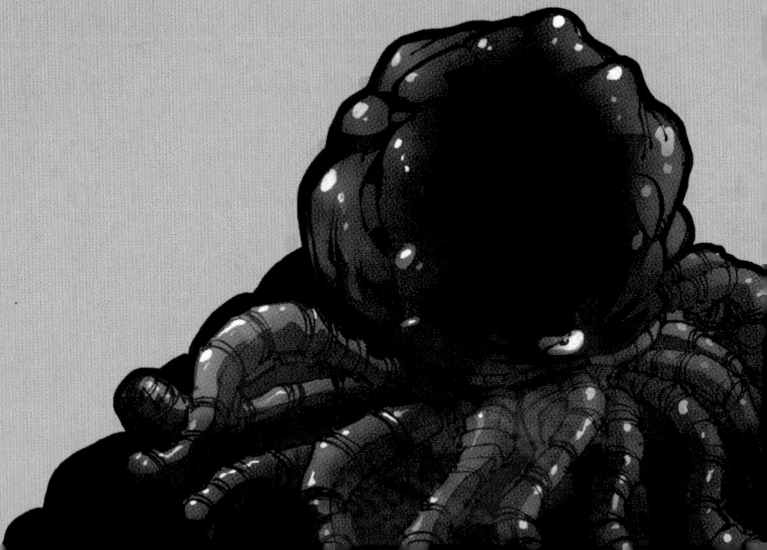

Other Books

The HOUND of the BASKERVILLES
by Sir Arthur Conan Doyle
retold by Martin Powell
GRAPHIC NOVEL
STONE ARCH Classic Fiction

The Hound of the Baskervilles

Late one night, Sir Charles Baskerville is attacked outside his castle in Dartmoor, England. Could it be the Hound of the Baskervilles, a legendary creature that haunts the nearby moor? Sherlock Holmes, the world's greatest detective, is on the case.

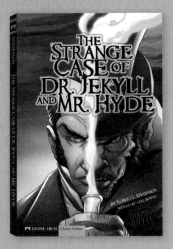

THE STRANGE CASE OF DR. JEKYLL AND MR. HYDE
BY ROBERT L. STEVENSON
RETOLD BY CARL BOWEN
GRAPHIC NOVEL
STONE ARCH Classic Fiction

The Strange Case of Dr. Jekyll and Mr. Hyde

Scientist Dr. Henry Jekyll believes every human has two minds: one good and one evil. He develops a potion to separate them from each other. Soon, his evil mind takes over, and Dr. Jekyll becomes a hideous fiend known as Mr. Hyde.

THE SWISS FAMILY ROBINSON
BY Johann D. Wyss
RETOLD BY MARTIN POWELL
WYSS THE SWISS FAMILY ROBINSON
STONE ARCH Classic Fiction

The Swiss Family Robinson

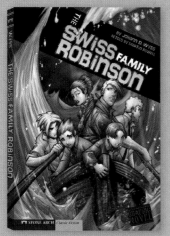

A family from Switzerland is shipwrecked on a deserted island. They discover that the island is filled with plants and animals they've never seen before. Unfortunately, not all of the creatures are friendly.

THE LEGEND OF SLEEPY HOLLOW
GRAPHIC NOVEL
STONE ARCH Classic Fiction

The Legend of Sleepy Hollow

A headless horseman haunts Sleepy Hollow! At least that's the legend in the tiny village of Tarry Town. But scary stories won't stop the town's new schoolmaster, Ichabod Crane, from crossing through the Hollow, especially when the beautiful Katrina Balt lives on the other side. Will Ichabod win over his beloved or discover that the legend of Sleepy Hollow is actually true?.

Internet Sites

Do you want to know more about subjects related to this book? Or are you interested in learning about other topics? Then check out FactHound, a fun, easy way to find Internet sites.

Our investigative staff has already sniffed out great sites for you!

Here's how to use FactHound:

1. Visit **www.facthound.com**
2. Select your grade level.
3. To learn more about subjects related to this book, type in the book's ISBN number: **9781434207579.**
4. Click the Fetch It button.

FactHound will fetch the best Internet sites for you!